THE LOST SUMMER

by

Robbie Moffat

PALM TREE PUBLISHING

PALM TREE PUBLISHING
Paisley, Scotland Pa1 1TJ

© Robbie Moffat 2017-2019

First published SEPTEMBER 2017
First published in paperback JANUARY 2109

Typeset: Verdana 8pt

ISBN-10: 0 907282547
ISBN-13: 978-0907282549

DEDICATION

This book is dedicated to everyone in Iceland who inspired me to write about them, or because of them. Thank you.

PREFACE

The setting for the story is the Western Fjords of Iceland, a peninsula that juts out into the cold waters two hundred miles east of Greenland. At the most westerly point of Europe and half a degree south of the Arctic Circle, the Fjords are remote and reached by sea or air. Only in the short summer months are the Fjords accessible by road.

The characters in this story all bear a resemblance to living people who resided in the small fjord town prior to the avalanche that destroyed much of the town in 1995.

<u>1</u>

Martin was standing on a chair as the ship ploughed through the North Sea swell. His hair was wet ... well, it had been.

"It should work!"

He was poking two bare wires into the only socket in the cabin.

Nothing happened.

Nothing had happened for the past hour since he had got out the shower and begun fiddling with the wires that were connected to his hairdryer.

"Your hair's dry, man" I snapped.

"No, no, it'll work..."

No-one could ever say that Mart wasn't persistent. But perched on a chair on a rolling North Sea ferry? For an hour?

"Lie down, man, lie down ... you're bloody crazy."

I mean, his hair was dry, yet there he was still trying to get his hair drier to go. He was swaying backwards and forwards, and it was making me sick.

"See, Jim..." He showed me the dryer.

"The things's going backwards. What good is that then? It's sucking air in instead of blowing it out. Give it a miss."

He looked sort of sheepish but remained there for a couple of minutes before getting down off the chair.

He climbed up into the top bunk above me.

"That's nice" he sighed.

Mart lay there overhead, thinking. I lay below trying to work out what he was thinking. We were two hours out of Aberdeen. For the first time in ages, I was just starting to relax. I began to remember some of the things that had happened since we had left Somerset. I was in the process of recapturing the tranquility of Cothelstone, when Mart suddenly climbed down from his bunk.

"I think I'll do some washing."

"Johnny Jesus, Mart...." I mean, he'd only been on his back about two minutes and there he was up again washing his underwear and socks. I glared at him ... but he just shrugged his shoulders and gave me a shy smile.

See, Martin has the sort of smile that melts hostility. I'm not sure how he does it, maybe it's from years of constantly pissing people off. It's amazing. I'd be just about ready to get really annoyed by his fidgeting, and whoosh ... he'd cock his head and look at me with such an innocent look, I'd go all soft.

That's how it's always been with Mart, ever since I met him in Joburg a few weeks before they threw Biko out of the sixth floor window of the BOSS building. Yip, we were there, and he wasn't the only black-boy that that happened to. The cops had the street below the building cordoned off from time to time. It was almost like a public execution, and everyone knew it. Or at least that's how I remember it.

In Johannesburg, Mart and I were both living in the same commune on Soper Road, and South Africa being the place it was, I reckon it was the only commune in the whole country at the time. We were lepers, social outcasts. We couldn't find work. We couldn't make friends except for the dozen or so folks we shared the commune with. Sure, no big deal, most of them were traveling people, and for sure, most of us agreed that the Transvaal was nearer hell than limbo.

And here, eleven years later, were Mart and me, setting out on a money making trip to Iceland. We were certainly no more settled or wealthier, and probably even less secure in ourselves than we were in Joburg. We'd both got a little older, but with even less to lose. I'd just spent three months in Thailand and Indonesia, and I'll admit that it was great. I can't think of anything better than to snooze in a hammock strung from a palm tree.

Mart had just come up from Elat on the Red Sea after some time in Brazil. He's spent a couple of weeks in Ireland before coming to stay with me at my cottage in Somerset. My rented cottage.

Martin had brought three weeks of rain with him, and between bouts of booze and soft drugs, we decided that if the summer were going to be so miserable, we'd quit England.

I was getting moved on anyway. The squire wanted the cottage for the gamekeeper, which was fair enough as he wanted to rear six thousand pheasants for the shooting season. I had been planning to bugger off to the States to see some pals, but I'd lost my motivation.

The problem was ... I was broke. I had run up debts getting on for five thousand pounds, which was hardly surprising, as I hadn't worked for six months. I was on the verge of what the legal men call bankruptcy, and I had to do something if I was going to stay out of the courts. Sure, I had no intention of running out on my debts, I have scruples ... but five thousand is a lot to pay back when you've nothing to show for it. There was no point in getting a labouring job in England, for even if I saved fifty pounds a week, it'd take me three years to pay it back once the interest was added on.

Nope, labouring was the dope's way. Sure thing, I could go to the States, but the States isn't a good place to start off broke. I'd done my share of cotton picking and store-to-store salesmanship. I had an opening to drive cab in San Francisco as I'd done it before, but I knew if I went to The Bay, I'd spend all my dough on renting an apartment and keeping away from cocaine.

So, when Mart showed up and said that he had to find two thousand for a nose operation in October and that he wanted another thousand to pay his solicitor to sort out his ninety thousand dollar debts in Australia (where he had three kids by his first wife and a joint owned house in downtown Sydney), we decided that the best thing we could do was work the fish in Iceland.

It all sounds crazy.... not the fishing, the rest of it, the whole damn crazy way we live. Between Mart and me, we'd been to most of the countries in the world. Two hundred? Two hundred and ten? I've been to seventy, and Mart's been to one hundred and fifty. Give or take an overlap, that's about fifty extra countries no-one has heard of.

We left Somerset four days ago. It had taken me a long time to pack my belongings on account of the weather. After the three weeks of rain Mart brought, we had two weeks of heat wave. The cottage at Cothelstone was a suntrap. If I were to describe the beauty of the place, then you might ask why I left it behind. Perhaps it is sufficient to say that Cothelstone remains one of the most beautiful places I've been. Maybe you can't believe that there are places in England that can sustain upper eighty degree weather day after day, even soar into the nineties.... but there are, and it does, and its the truth.

Anyway, Martin restructured my bookshelves to make a trunk to throw my clothes into. We had written off to companies in Iceland and were waiting to hear. A letter arrived and we were on our way. I hired a van; we loaded up my belongings, and drove overnight the four hundred miles to Glasgow.

Early morning we arrived at my parents council house, slept the afternoon, unloaded the van in the evening, then leaving Mart in Glasgow, I drove back down to Somerset and dropped the van off at eight in the morning. Two hours later I was on a bus back to Glasgow and back there by five.

Following morning, my brother-in-law Sandy took Mart and I the hundred fifty miles north to Banchory where we connected with Jake.

Jake was an old mate of mine that went back to my Newcastle days.

"Iceland! What the hell are you going to Iceland for?"

"Scotland's Iceland's nearest neighbour."

"It's for money" Mart corrected me.

The truth is, I don't really want to tell you this story. It's painful. I'd rather just get on and write some poetry or something. I'm happy when I write poetry. I think I'm a poet, but that doesn't mean that I am. Poetry's my hobby. Everyone's got a hobby or at least something, which interests him or her, more than anything else. Mart's hobby is women, or at least, that's what he spends most of his time talking and dreaming about. In our one night in Banchory, he took up with Hurricane Heather (well, that was his nickname for her). It meant I got the spare double bed at Jake's cottage to myself. The following afternoon we were in Aberdeen, and at six, Jake stood waving on the quay as we shipped out of the harbour for Lerwick.

"Well, Jim, we're on our way. I'm glad we're going by boat and not by plane."

Here's another truth. It didn't cost much more to fly to Iceland, but I couldn't put the money up front. Mart and I were traveling on credit, my credit. But this story's not really about being a bum and getting further into debt. I'm not the main character, the kingpin of the drama. This story's about Martin.

See, I just want to tell you about my mate ... my friend who has been so many places and done so many things that you won't believe half of it. Sure, you always have to take the things Mart says with a pinch of salt, and after all, there are few good story tellers who don't embellish their tall tales or enhance the glamour of their romances.... but whether Mart is talking about milking snakes or getting lost on horseback in the Australian desert, there's some thread of truth in his stories. Mart doesn't really need to spin a web of fiction; his fact is the fiction of boys' adventure books.

To look at Mart, you might think that he had been a boxer some time back. His nose is as flat as a flounder's belly. He's broken it a couple of times and I've never found out how. Over abuse of cocaine has done the rest to damage it from the inside so that he has the habit of sniffing all the time.

Maybe it's not a habit; maybe it's the only way he can keep the air passage open. I'm not going to speculate. Mart's sensitive about his nose and I never really felt getting too personal about it. He obviously worried about it. By working in Iceland, he had the chance of paying for the operation that would give him a new nose.

It might seem laughable, but Mart's nose sure put a lot of people off him. It made him look as though he'd hung around with the wrong sort of guys who eventually had done him over.

Mart's reason for going to Iceland to earn money seemed a lot more worthy than mine. I needed the money to pay off my credit cards. I'd been running them up for years, and having run them up and over, way over, I had to pay up or run. Going to Iceland was a bit of both.

Whatever the outcome of our journey, money was the objective. But between you and me, I've never gone anywhere with Mart that has not ended up in some crazy deal or other. When you rove the world foot loose and fancy free, you get into things you'd steer clear off like the plague if you were home.

Whatever morals you have or cherish in your home country or town, leave them there. When you go to another country, it's another culture with other values. I'm not saying that Mart and I have a Viking mentality ... rape and plunder, that sort of thing, as soon as you touch distant shores. That's a crazy dream in times like now.

No, all I'm saying is, it's easy to go off the rails. It's easy to become lawless.

So there we were, Mart and me, on the ferry to Iceland. It was four days after the summer solstice. It was midnight. We were south of the Orkneys, and it was just getting dark. We were headed for a place half a degree south of the Arctic Circle where in summer there was no night. We didn't have a clue what we were letting ourselves in for.

<u>2</u>

Lerwick was freezing.

"It's bloody summer. What the hell am I doing in the Shetlands?"

Mart was shivering. He was wearing a yellow tee-shirt, a brown leather jacket, a pair of blue-jeans, a pair of black summer socks, and a pair of red sneakers … all the summer gear.

He had missed the heat wave.

"It was supposed to be seventy five degrees here," he moaned.

We were now closer to Bergen, Norway than Aberdeen. We had to change ferries in Lerwick. It was eight in the morning and we had an eighteen-hour wait. There was only one ferry a week to Iceland, the *Norvanna*. It took a week to do the round trip Bergen - Lerwick - Faroe - Iceland - Faroe - Lerwick - Esberg - Bergen. It only ran in the summer.

We left the quay side and headed into the town. Mart was full of memories.

"I've been here before. I was here in the Seventies."

Some workmen were digging up the road and we had to go round them. I'd been to Lerwick before the oil had arrived and chased off all the seagulls. Now the seagulls were back.

"I came here because I thought I could live here."

I gave Mart a worried look. I mean, no offense to the people of Lerwick, but who in their right mind would want to live sixty degrees north of the equator unless they were born there.

"When I got here, I realised it was a crazy idea. There were no trees. That's about all I remember. I stayed five days. I was a bit mixed up, I'd just left Australia and I didn't fancy living in London or England. I wanted to go north. I thought about Iceland, but I knew it'd be a lot warmer here. I wanted to do some hiking, but all I did was drink a lot."

It really was freezing. It couldn't have been more than eight or nine Celsius. And it was June.

"When I left here, I went back down to London. I'd got a cheap return ... and anyway, I had plenty of dosh. I'd been working in the desert for a year."

"The ranching you told me about? That time with the horse?"

"No.... I was piping ... an oil-line. I flew to London from Darwin. Stopped off in Bali first."

Bali. I'd been there in April. I'd got from Bangkok

all the way to Lombok before I turned around. I hadn't fancied going on to Australia. Silly bugger. If I had, I wouldn't have been on my way to Iceland.

For the first time in six months, I had put on a coat. The locals were going about their business, and groups of tourists were wandering up and down the narrow cobbled main street. Mart was shivering.

"I'm cold."

It was a bleak day. I looked back towards the harbour. Gulls and skeeters were swooping about in the 'summer din'. That's what the locals call the summer light. In many ways, Lerwick's a picturesque little town. But the oilmen have gone, and the town has sort of gone back to the way it was in '70. There was a 'cauld win' blawin', and I thought that the place hadn't changed all that much since I'd first visited it as a boy. I'm not saying that I've been to Lerwick a lot, but I've had occasions to go there for one reason or another. The islanders still haven't made any great effort to plant trees. Surely oil could have paid for it. Here and there behind the protection of a dyke, there was a fir or an elm or an oak, and no more. The rest was all grass and rock and lichen. Nothing else will grow as long as sheep are grazed on open pasture.

To pass the time, Mart and I walked out to

Clickimin Broch ... the Pict Castle on the edge of town. The broch was built about the same time as the Parthenon on the Acropolis, though Clickimin was first inhabited about the time the first pyramid was built. So while the Egyptians and the Greeks were busy running around terrorising the known world, the inhabitants of Clickimin just got on with their fishing and farming. Who knows what great chieftains had led the locals, and who knows what great wanderers set foot in the turf-topped burrows of the broch, but between you and me, as Mart and I weaved and crawled in and out the warren of tunnels, the schist walls spoke more tales to me than the inside of Cheops pyramid ever did.

Cheop's pyramid is just a tomb that one great man built in the hope of securing immortality. When you go inside Cheop's, there's that inexplicable lifelessness that all mausoleums have. But inside Clickimin, where mortals dwelt, there's a vitality and life that lives on.

I was so caught up in the 'spirits' of the broch, I hadn't noticed that Mart had disappeared. I climbed over the top of the castle and found him sitting by the edge of the lochan in a patch of wild orchids, white star and forget-me-nots. Brilliantly fluorescent clumps of buttercup grew out of moss layered stone that had first been placed there as a sea-wall by bronze-age man.

"This is an old place, Jim..... I like it."

Beyond the broch, the swell of fish and kelp and peat and salt lured us to the shore of Brei Wick where we struggled with our boredom by peering into wrack pools and shells and urchins smashed open and eaten by gulls. Mart chased two white-bellied crows with a 'Caaawww!" that echoed across the water.

Mart had a habit of communicating with animals and creatures in a guttural fashion that usually chased them off. It was a game with him that sent flocks of sheep off on the run. It amused him. Yet when he wished to, he could creep up on birds and catch them in his hands, or disappear into the long grass and emerge with a snake or a sloe-worm. At Cothelstone, he would vanish into the undergrowth and reappear hours later with stories of a jay he'd caught or about a fox and pheasant fight he's seen or about a poor rabbit he'd had to put out of it's misery because it had been hit by a car.

Mart, even with all his traveling, was an explorer by nature. One day he went rummaging in a farm out-house no one had been in for twenty years and emerged with a stuffed gannet and a penny-farthing wheel.

Live gannets and kittiwakes slew about in the Shetland wind. The day was passing slowly. There wasn't much to do and endless cups of tea in the different town cafes wore us out. We tried to sleep on the grass lawn of Charlotte Castle, but it was impossible. It was cold and the bloody gannets made such a noise; we started wandering the grey granite streets again. We stopped and asked the town traffic warden the time.

"Five to two."

We got talking.

"So you play the guitar or fiddle...?" Mart asked.

"A bit of baeth."

"Is that right" I said. "There can't be too many singing traffic wardens in Lerwick."

"Och, no, I'm the only ane in Shetland and Orkneys."

Mart was looking at the numeral on the warden's lapel.

"How come you're number 2?" he queried.

"Och, everone asks that. See, there's ane polis'man living here wi' the number 462, but there's anely three polis'men in the Isles. When the traffic ward'an in Inverness died, they gave the vacant post tae the Shetland County Council. We'd waited years tae have our turn. See, they're only allowed tae issue so many in the Highlands and Islands. The number comes wi' the job. I think that's how it is anyway. But it's nae a job really ... ma work starts when I finish."

"How's that then?" I asked

"Life starts when work finishes" Mart said, shuffling restlessly. He was ready for another cup of tea.

"Aye, that's true. Ma real work is singing and playing. I make quite a bit in the summer months in the hotels wi' the tourists."

"You write your own songs then?" I was hoping he was a poet and that we had something in common.

"A few ... a tune frae this ... a few lines of ma ane, a few words frae some old song. The ballad tradition. A bit of this and that and I make it ma ane."

We parted company, but we saw him everywhere after that. Lerwick's a very small place. We saw dozens of the same people dozens of times all day.

We counted the number of names listed on the Great War memorial.

"Six hundred and forty" I declared.

"I lost count" said Mart. "There's only twenty thousand people here in the Shetlands now. Six hundred and forty dead? Christ, that must have been a crazy war. These six hundred and forty must have been nearly all the young men on the isles. You'll never get me in an army fighting for stupid things."

I had to say something.

"We're just lucky we don't have to fight. They did it all for us, these guys."

"They did it for themselves, the silly buggers. And look where it got them. Yeah, we're lucky.... we get to work in Iceland."

I groaned.

We took shelter in the library museum. It seemed that the only warm places in Lerwick were sites of historical interest or places with information on sites of interesting history. In the library it was cosy and we hid behind big volumes of portrait photography and slept.

We were not the only ones.

"My name's Sunni" she whispered to Mart.

"Oh, pleased to meet you. This is my mate, Jim."

Sunni was from Copenhagen. She was waiting for the *Noranna* too. She was going to the Faroes, heaven knows what for, until we found out that she was on vacation for a week. It was summer after all, though looking out the window at the grey clouds swirling about the Lerwick sky, we were convinced that Scandinavian summer didn't mean that it couldn't snow.

The library closed at five and Suni took refuge with us in the bakery cafe on Commercial Street. We played matchsticks over cups of tea and ended up in the Seamen's Mission teaching Sunni how to play pool. We soon found out that she'd played before when she beat us both.

There was something about Sunni that .... well, I was attracted to her. So was Mart, but then again, Mart's attracted to any girl that show's any amount of interest in him. If a girl talks to him, that's enough, Mart assumes that she's fair game. I'm not being unfair, I know Mart, and I know that both of us wanted to lay our hands on Sunni. She wasn't the best looking girl in world, as if that mattered anyway, she was a nice girl, but we controlled ourselves. She went off someplace else, and Mart and I retreated to the sit-in chip shop in a hungry state.

"You can have her," I said to him.

"No," he replied, "be my guest. She's yours. I had Hurricane Heather two nights ago, remember."

We were discussing Sunni as if she didn't have a

mind of her own. The truth was that both of us were only half-interested in trying a seduction routine once we were aboard ship. It was lust that drove us on, but self-respect that held us back.

We were halfway through our haddocks before I was on the make. I was eying up a girl in the corner. Mart had managed to catch the attention of a middle-aged couple from Utah.

"We've only been here week, bud. You couldn't suggest some real good places to see in the Shetland Islands here?"

"God," Mart whispered to me in an aside "we've done the impossible. We've managed to fool someone into thinking that we're local." He turned to the Americans. "Och, my memories not what it used to be? I left here when I was seventeen and I've only just come back after twenty years to bury my grandmother."

"Really?" the couple said with some sympathy.

"Aye ... Hear that?" In the games room of the chip-shop, some teenager was playing a slot machine. The machine was playing a tune as it paid out. "There's a boy in there getting paid for performing."

Another ten pence dropped.

"We don't have them in Utah" the American man

said.

"Are children allowed to play them?" the woman inquired.

"Aye" I replied, "It's mainly kids ... and the adults who don't grow up."

That was it the introductions were done. Pretty soon they were telling us about Vegas. They lived a four-hour drive away. We didn't dare tell them that both of us had been there.

Time was dripping like water from a tap. I kept catching the eye of the pretty girl in the corner. Mart's eyes were drooping. He was worn out. He'd had three straight nights on the booze ... Glasgow ... Banchory ... and the ferry from Aberdeen. He'd had twelve hours sleep. So had I.

Over Mart's shoulder the girl in the corner was studying a map of the Faroe. It was obvious where she was going.

"You waiting for the boat too, sweetheart?"

I was in. We got talking quickly and intently. Within ten minutes I was asking her if she would come and live with me in Banchory when I got back from Iceland.

Martin nearly fell off his chair.

Her name was Gilla.

She was from Brunswick, Germany, and had been to Scotland fourteen times.

3

The fog horn is sounding out into the Atlantic mist. Faroe lies six hours behind us and east Iceland eight hours before us.

In Torshun, Martin said goodbye to Lunni and I to Gilla, the German girl I first saw in the fish and chip shop. It is a far cry from meetings and affairs under the palm trees in some southern paradise.

But, all that was days before. Martin is lost in the mountains of Iceland. I wait for him by the hotel window that gives a view of snow-covered slopes and cums. We had set off along the beach towards the old whaling station a mile out of Flateyri. We found whalebone and discarded harpoon hafts in an abandoned beach shed. Beyond that place we dug remains in the ruins of dwellings once lived in with stone and roofed with peat which stood three feet from the high tide line. We hoped for a whale tooth or an old fishing hook, but we found nothing.

Now, I am worried! Martin has been in the mountains five hours. I had been digging in a dwelling further up the hill from the whaling station, when he shouted to me,

"I'm going back a different way."

I nodded and watched as he headed up the mountain. At first it seemed he was following the fence of a farm which he could round and then strike off back towards Flateyri along the foot of the mountains. But no. He began to climb.

I sat and watched for twenty minutes and he

continued to climb. The slope was one in three and a little higher became one in two. Above were thousand foot basalt cliffs.

I thought him crazy. He had set off up a part of the mountain that would leave him stranded in scree. I watched and anticipated that the only option he would have was to strike westwards along a ridge of cliff which would take him towards the safety of a cum. I sat there and watched him become a dot. At about eight hundred feet he struck off to the west as anticipated.

I set out to head him off. I went west a quarter of a mile and then took a north west bearing so that I would reach the cum before him if I climbed steady.

The climb took about an hour, and for the second half hour I expected to see Martin come over the ridge to my east. I thought that he'd be some hundreds of feet above me, but his lateral climb would mean that I would soon reach the same height and be ahead by two hundred yards or more.

To avoid the scree, I had to climb higher and higher and higher until eventually I reached a spur that looked hundreds of feet down into the ice cratered cum. The mountain peak lay three hundred feet above me. I stripped off and lay semi-naked in the saxifrage and lichens and waited for Martin. The blue ford mountains rimmed with snow hemmed the horn-shaped spit and the town of Flateyri jagging out into the dark blue water … the sea and the clear white horizon of the Denmark Strait and beyond which lay the shore of Greenland. All this was beneath me …

small enclosed fields and the few farm houses that are ribboned along the ford … the white sand deposited on the ness by the sea, the black sand and the pebbles thrown on the sea by the crumbling basalt mountains … all of this and the sun … this was my new home in Iceland.

Out of the wind, it was twenty-five Celsius … sixty-six degrees north, just half a degree south of the Arctic Circle. There was snow, but there were streams and wheatears and curlews and buntings. But up in the cum there were only wheatears, white and brown marked creatures with a shrill cry.

I waited for Martin. He did not show. I climbed higher to see if I could catch sight of him, but I saw nothing. Only great runs of scree rushing a thousand feet down the mountain.

I gazed at the peak. I had only eaten once and it was four o'clock. To climb to the top alone, without food or water, and then to descend hungry and tired … I decided that it would be foolhardy to push my luck. The cliffs crumbled at the slightest touch. Sure, it wasn't far to the top, but it never is when you're three-quarters there. No, it was best I climb down into the cum and explore it rather than risk my neck on the cliffs.

In the cum I was alone. There were no wheaters, only silence. The cliffs horseshoed around me. It was a quarter mile from side to side and was a natural amphitheater filled with snow and boulders. I addressed my audience.

"I … am … told … that … man … believes … that

… he … alone … possesses … the … world … If … this … then … is … man, … against … all … convention … I … will… not … be … the … man … I … will … be."

It wasn't a great speech but the echo was amazing. If I pitched my voice on to the eastern wall of the cum which had not eroded and become blanketed in scree like the south and west walls I could amplify my voice a hundred fold. I sat on a large rock in the centre of the cum and practised my alphabet. I discovered that my B, C, G, and P were not very clear because of the nature of my pronunciation. There was no echo. I practised B, C, G, P until they resounded.

I wrote my name in the ice.

But where was Martin? I was worried thought I knew he had a cat's life. I descended to the lip of the cum and once again scanned the mountainside for him.

Nothing.

Half an hour later I was at the foot of the mountain and on the road back into Flateyri. Again and again I scanned for Martin. Either he had climbed to the top and gone over the ridge or he had fallen. Instinct made me believe the latter, but as I had no idea where he was, I returned to the town where I watched from the hotel window.

An hour later I am growing anxious. If Martin is lost in the mountains then I will need to gather some people to search for him. It is silly to go alone. If he is injured I want to be able to carry him down unaided.

What was that? A knock? A tap?

"I fell on the mountain."

It was Martin, red-faced and with a can of low-alcohol Icelandic beer in his hand.

"I fell forty feet. I lay there for an hour and a half hoping you'd find me. I was right near the top, I nearly got there."

"You silly bugger. There was no way I was following you up the route you took. I thought you were going to traverse across the ridge."

"I went straight up."

"I waited for you. I knew that where you went up couldn't be climbed."

"It looked easy. I nearly got to the top but the rock kept coming loose."

"Scree's the most dangerous thing to climb. I learned that when I was fifteen. Once you start falling you keep going. If you turn head over, you've had it. If you keep feet first, you've a chance, you might only get a broken back."

"I was trying to get over my fear of heights. I fell once before. I thought if I climbed to the top I'd be okay again."

"It's not the way to do it. You shouldn't have gone up that way. You didn't even tell me what you were doing."

"It looked so easy. I'll never go climbing again."

"Never do it alone. Always do it in twos. And pick your route before you start, for once you're up there, you better be sure you can get back down"

The lesson was over. I hadn't taught it, Martin

had learned it all for himself.

4

Day is night and night is day, it doesn't matter. It is never dark.

Martin and I share a room in a communal house for factory workers. Everything is paid for by the company. There are no bills, no need to replace light bulbs or buy toilet paper. Everything is supplied … except food.

Oddahus stands by the fish factory at the end of the spit that is Flateyri. Fifty yards in and in three directions is the fjord. From every window except from mine, there is a view of water and mountains. My window overlooks the side of the factory. To the left I can see the mouth of the fjord and the Arctic Ocean beyond, and above the factory roof I get a glimpse of the ice capped mountains.

Every mountain has a name and as time passes perhaps I will learn to know them. We have settled into the house and already Martin has found himself a friend. Her name is Claire and he has set about converting her. She is a lesbian and shows Martin nude photographs of her lesbian friends. They sit and discuss genital sizes and Claire shows Martin her cunt. But he is not allowed to touch.

Claire lives in the room next to us. She is from South Africa and hasn't been there for years. She's been in Iceland two years and before that she was in Israel for three. She's a stateless person. She is saving up her fish money to start up a business. "What sort of business?" She doesn't know. She's very mixed up but Martin's working on opening her out, trying to get in her pants. She's a plain sort of girl with deep set eyes. She's very lonely and not very well liked. She can speak a little Icelandic and came to Flateyri from another factory in Keflavik where she wasn't getting along with people. Martin has instantly become her closest friend.

"Maybe I'll get to sleep with Claire tonight."

"Oh yeah."

"We've got a double bed now."

"A double bed? Where did that come from?"

"We put two singles together."

"Oh ..."

Martin is sex crazed. He'll chase anything. I mean it. He's a lover boy who'll love anybody. Maybe that's not such a bad thing. It seems to make life less complicated. Martin says he's never told any woman that he loved her and he doubts very much that he's ever been in love. In the last year he'd been to bed with more than fifty women. I reckon that's about the sum total of my whole sex life. But see he never seems to hang on to them. I reckon that with most of his conquests it's the conquest and not the desire for possession that motivates him. Once he's been to bed with them his interest wears. I guess that's why marriage isn't sacred to him, getting married is just like getting laid.

Martin is a polygamist. He's done it more than twice. Martin's been married five times and not been divorced once. "I mean it's a different country each time. It doesn't matter."

"What do you mean it doesn't matter?"

"It's nothing."

"Jesus, man, what about the poor women? Do they know?"

"It doesn't matter!"

"Why do you keep getting married? To make the women you're fucking feel better?"

"It makes me feel better. I can live in Tonga, Australia, Brazil …"

"And now you're in bloody Iceland."

"Claire and I are going to go to Amsterdam together in September."

"You're crazy. She's really strange."

"I know that. I can help her. I'm stranger than she is. I've changed her already. She's been much happier since I've been here. She told me that. She's into whips and that. She's got a suitcase of dirty mags. But they're nothing. I tell her that. In Amsterdam they're really dirt."

Sex mad. With Claire he's found someone who shares the same interest … women. All he's got to do is become a woman and maybe Claire will fuck him.

This is the way life is. I'm not going to lie to you. The world is full of weirdos and Martin's definitely one of them. The thing is, he's a friend of mine and that makes all the difference. Deep down, he's a good guy. Sometimes he can be a bit of a vacuum cleaner … give him something to sip or nibble and he'll consume the lot. He's not got a single measure of self control. He's epicurean through and through. If something gives him pleasure, then he can't get enough of it. He can't get enough sex, but who can anyway?

I haven't had any for two months, that's about the longest for ten years. But that's my choice. Sex comes easy if you put out the feelers. Flateyri is full of hot Icelandic girls. I'm not going to make any excuses, there was too many women in my life earlier in the year. That's one reason I fled off to Thailand in January. I was living with one girl, having a relationship with another a hundred miles away, and ran away to south-east Asia with a third. Meanwhile I was going through the process of divorce. See, I'm not like Martin, I believe in marriage and I suppose that makes me a boring old fart. Who cares? Maybe I need the security of knowing that there are women who love me and not fifty who just want to fuck me. I'm pretty much a monogamous sort of guy (except for the phase I just went through). Martin is not, he'll cheat on anyone, and give himself to nobody. He doesn't give a toss for love, it's all lust. By contrast, I go for love and try to make my lust respectable. In a way I envy Martin's approach, but in another I feel sorry for him. He never holds out for the girl he really wants, he takes the first one that comes along, then works his way through the pack. I tend to bide my time, go for the one I want, and stick with her. Martin might fuck fifty women once while I fuck one fifty times. It sort of evens out. One thing it straightens out … I'm not interested in his women and he never gets to screw mine.

Does all this sound macho? Well, that's the

plain truth. Martin and I are men, and I don't know any men who think any different when it comes to women. When it comes down to it, we are all animals, and everyone knows that animals have more fun. People who deny themselves sex are nearly always miserable. Martin is downright miserable when he hasn't had any for a week or two.

Maybe I should tell you about some of the other folk who live in the 'workhouse' with us. But not now, 'cause I've more to say about Martin.

At work, Martin is a lazy sod. If there's an easy job he'll find it and not let anyone else have it. He stops to roll a fag every twenty minutes or so. When we were at Cothelstone he never used to smoke that much, maybe half an ounce every two days. In the factory he's on an ounce a day. Sure, I have the odd one now and then but that doesn't make much difference. Guess I can hardly say no to cigarettes, and it's easy when you don't buy them. Having a pouch of tabs or a pouch of baccy in your pocket just makes the hands itch for a smoke. That's the way it is with Mart. He'll have some boring job in the factory that isn't keeping him occupied and suddenly with his hands free he's out with the tobacco and rolling up. Next thing he's leaning against a wall taking a drag. When he gets like that I throw him a dirty look especially when the rest of us are working. His idleness just gives everyone else all the more work to do.

I try not to let it get to me. I just kind of shrug my shoulders and say "what the fuck" under my breath and get on with that I'm doing. Why should I be the one to let him know that he's fucking up? That's Goosti, the foreman's job. I just work in the place like everybody else.

Because Martin's always looking for the soft option in the factory he gets to work with the kids most of the time. The kids get paid less than we do. They're all working their way through the summer to pay for their schooling in Reykjavik. Kids get sent away from the age of twelve and being sent away to school in Iceland usually means Reykjavik. So kids start working in the factory at the age of twelve. People reckon that you should be fourteen, but nearly everybody who still works fish started when they were twelve. It sounds hard, but these kids get good money and they're good workers. Sure, they kid around and have fun and sometimes don't do a grown man or woman's work but they're kids, yet when the heat is on, they can work themselves into the guts and blood that's everywhere. Sometimes I look at them and Martin working together and think that the company's getting their money's worth from the kids but not from Martin. Most of the jobs he does, they'd do better employing another kid than having this guy from England-Australia or wherever working for them, doing very little every day yet still racking up the overtime because he doesn't clock out until almost the last worker has gone home.

Maybe I'm being unfair and prejudiced and harsh because I'm Martin's mate. I'm not saying he's an embarrassment to me, shit, we're all on our own in this world and without mates where would we be. What I feel though is that people see him as my friend and I can see that some of them kind of treat us as a pair. Nothing weird or anything like that, but we came together, we share a room, we're bonded. Thing is, we're far from that and after two weeks most people know that now. The girls aren't so sure and knowing the way Mart behaves with women, they probably think I'm sex crazed too.

But who cares.

Some mornings Mart wakes up hating the whole world. He curses and swears at everything but me, though maybe in his mind he's doing that too. Even though he doesn't buy milk or bread he'll curse the fact that there's none in the kitchen for coffee and toast. See, everything in the world is free to Martin. People just leave things lying around for him to use. If it's there, then no one wants it or has any use for it. That's why he always wants to lock our room door. Mart thinks that just because he picks things up other people do too. He doesn't trust people very much, and maybe that's because he thinks the world is a free for all where you've got to look after what you've got or you'll have nothing.

That is exactly what Mart has ... nothing. After thirty-eight years of giving away everything every time he acquired something he's got nothing. Maybe if he didn't have this habitual habit of walking out on people, and in particular the women he's lived with, then he'd come out of it with some material possessions. But TVs and stereos, and videos and washing machines and wardrobes of clothes are all replaceable to Martin. And so they are, but by having to replace all these things every time he settles down is like a reoccurring dream at the end of which he always wakes up with nothing.

Maybe that's not such a bad thing either. Too many people work their whole damn life for what … to let their kids auction off their house and furniture and spend it on fast cars and fast living once the folks have passed on. Sure, there are the majority of folk who are without a penny and without ever having had enough to put a penny in the bank and in a way Martin's no different from them. But see, Martin's not really contributing to the future, he only thinks for himself. I'm not saying he's selfish … well, maybe I am. Maybe he is self-centred and stingy and mean and always looking out for number one, but is he any different from you or me? I can't take a big moral stance and say that I'm working in the factory for Iceland's future. No way, I'm there to pay off my debts. Shit, I pay tax and I don't like it. No one likes paying tax, no one. It's a universal bugbear the world over. But I'm not going to go into that one here.

No, Martin's whole way of life is so different from mine. He's been hanging out with the Amsterdam underworld and some of the dishonesty and mistrust has attached itself to Mart. Sometimes it's hard to admit to myself that Mart is a shady character, not shifty, but not that honest. I mean, it's hard working out the fact from the fiction. He tends to exaggerate … he'd told Mike that we'd had an orgy in our room two nights ago. Mike told me, but I put him straight. We didn't have no orgy. Instead some horny little fifteen year old had got into bed with me and we had screwed. We were drunk and didn't care. Martin had passed out from over work as much as he had from the vodka. But me and Elin woke him up and all I remember is seeing him playing the peeping tom as we made love. I felt as though we were being spied on, but I was too drunk and too horny to let go of Elin. She held on even tighter.

Elin's pretty mixed up. She was seduced by her father when she was nine, then again when she was eleven and thirteen. Ever since that … well, she says that every time she screws a guy she's trying to relive her father. I mean, she's only fifteen and a half, and according to Mia everyone in the town knows about her and her dad.

Flateyri's one hell of a small town. Mart doesn't fit in. People kind of shun him because he's made a bad first impression. He's a pretty negative guy on occasions. No one wants to hang out with someone who moans all the time and Mart complains something evil! He calls people names like "cow", "bitch", "whore". See, Mart's whole conversation revolves around women. He don't dare call the guys "shits", or "cunts" 'cause they'd beat his brains out. I reckon Mart's a coward, but I don't see why.

The more I get to know Martin the more I think that he needs rehabilitating. He isn't cut out for the straight life of work and honesty. No one at the factory wants to work with him any more. If there's a job to be done and there's someone else around to do it he'll let them. Shit, the other day we were loading fifty kilo baskets of fish into two containers which were being shipped out to Mike's dad in Grimsby. There were two teams of five. Each team had one guy icing and two pairs of guys working together loading the bakkas into the container. I was working in one team and Mart the other and didn't have time to see what was going on with the other container, we were working solid.

Every hour we got a smoke break. When the factory bell went, we shuffled inside to get out of the wet misty morning. Martin usually always stops whatever he's doing a few minutes before the bell, and is always one of the last back to work. When we got back to the containers Goosti came and took away our icer and one of the pairs of guys. This left me and Bill, a South African guy who'd been at the factory for ten months. The container was getting near full and there was only room enough for one pair of guys to stack bakkas anyway, but we needed a guy to ice the fish for us as we loaded it in.

"Hey, Beggi ... want to come and ice for us."

"Ha ..." he said looking at Bill.

"Come on, Beggi ... give us a hand."

Beggi shook his head.

"Ekki mig ..." and said something about how he was with the other team.

"Yow ... Gummi," he shouted to Gummi. Gummi looked up and shook his head too.

"No way, man … no way."

Just then Mart came out of the factory with a rolly in his hand. He looked up and everyone looked the other way and laughed. There was no point in asking Mart to helps, we knew we'd be better off doing it ourselves.

See, that's the way the guys feel about Martin. He's not pulling his weight and that means that in a town like Flateyri he's a liability. For the factory is Flateyri. Half the town works in the factory or on the boats that supply the factory with fish. Without the factory, there'd be no Flateyri. That's why the kids work in the factory from the age of twelve or fourteen or whatever. They work with their fathers, mothers, brothers, sisters, cousins, in fact nearly everyone is some cousin or uncle or niece removed. It's a community, a fishing community that pulls together. Everyone has a stake in the work at the factory, everyone shares in the wealth it brings to the community.

Martin uses and abuses the community by doing as little work as possible, by taking longer breaks than everyone else.

I'm not going to go on and on. It's obvious that in a small place like Flateyri, it doesn't take the community long to work out what is good and what is bad for it.

I'm not saying that Mart isn't any good for a small town like Flateyri. All I'm saying is that Mart is struggling to survive. No one really likes him except Claire and besides Mart, Claire's probably the most disliked person in the factory. Maybe it's their dislike for everyone else that has thrown them together, two lost souls adrift in a country they're not coming to terms with. Icelanders dislike them because they have decided they don't like Icelanders.

Everyone to their own, but no one is ever going to have a good time in a foreign country if they go around swearing at everyone and everything.

With Mart that's starting to stop now as the reverse has taken place, everyone curses him.

<u>5</u>

So it snowed. Sure, it's July and it's Iceland …
but snow?

"It's been a lousy summer."

Aegil took his rifle and shot a seagull. It fell
from the grey sky and plunged into the sea. It floated
on the dark Arctic waters.

"So the government pays twenty kroner a kilo."

"Yawl … we take them over to the fox farm in
Isafirdi where they weight them and pay us. It's got
to be done. Stinking seals give the cod worms."

Maybe it sounds crazy, maybe I'm making
excuses for killing, but as I've said, the fish are
everything in Iceland.

We were on a seal hunt. We'd taken a line boat
out of the fjord and turned southwards along the coast
after we'd reached the sea. Aegil pointed to an
enormous fork of cloud to the west.

"That's Greenland over there. Can't see nothing
…"

The sea was as smooth as glass. There was no
swell … not even a white top. It was as calm as any
sea I'd ever seen.

We'd left Martin in Flateyri. He wasn't invited
on the hunt, maybe because Aegil didn't like him very
much. Aegil was the guy who had written back to us
when we'd applied for the job. He'd been the one to
give us the work. If we had any problem we took
them to Aegil. He was one of our bosses, but he
wasn't like any boss I'd ever had.

Aegil was a character out of fiction. He was tall, real tall, with cropped blond hair. He was a born hunter without being mean or brutal. Sure, he killed for sport. Shooting seagulls was no big thing. His azure eyes narrowed and he squeezed the trigger. There was no thought of gulls being fellow creatures on this planet. He and them were in competition. The birds got fat and ugly on the fish. Thousands of them.

"See those cliffs there … they say that there are about one quarter million gulls living there and eating the cod! We feed them too. They hang out around the factory just waiting to be fed. Every year there's more of them."

I'd never seen so many gulls. The sky was thick with them … black-eyed creatures that swooped so close to the boat that you could see their minds working. They watches us and showed no fear. The bang … a bullet would take them out, half kill them so that once down on the water they'd have to be shot again, and then maybe again until they floated spread winged head down and lifeless.

We left a wake of dead gulls along the coast until we all came to a place where we were going to put ashore in Bjam's small dinghy we had in tow.

Bjam was crazy. He had been married the weekend before. He wasn't a good looking guy, his buttocks hung out of his pants when he went over. But looks aren't everything and he was a friendly bloke. He had a devilish grin when he got a gull in the sights of his Winchester. He'd pump away and not really care if he hit a bird. Occasionally he'd fire from the hip as if he was some kind of maverick. He'd whoop and holler and who's to say that what he was doing wasn't harmless. He didn't get to go seal hunting much, maybe a couple of times a year.

Aegil tried to go hunting every Sunday. He was the genuine thing and everyone knew it. The day before, we'd all been drunk and driven into Isafirdi to the dance. I'd bought the kids some drinks in the bar and been arrested for supplying minors with liquor. The kids had been eighteen and I hadn't known that they had to be twenty to have booze in an Icelandic bar. The cops kept me at the station for an hour and a half. They were nice enough guys and I got to watch the movie *Tora Tora Tora* with them on the box. Even they shook their heads at how crazy the kamikazes were. They eventually let me go and took me back to the dance.

I was pretty far gone. I'd had half a bottle of whiskey in the afternoon and three-quarters of a bottle of vodka in the evening, plus more whiskey and wine and God knows what else. I ended up in the back of the return taxi to Flateyri with a woman that Aegil later told me was crazy and looking for a husband. I thought she was alright but Mike told me that I'd been too drunk to know what I was doing.

I guess these things happen.

So here we were eight hours later getting out the line boat into the dinghy to go ashore. As we came to the beach we were grounded on some rocks and as Aegil tried to steer us ashore with the oar, it snapped.

It was to be one of those days. The seals would pop up out of the water. Aegil would aim and fire, then nothing … we'd wait to see if the seal would resurface. Fifteen, twenty minutes. We'd move off along the beach but every time Aegil fired at a seal, there would be a splash and the seal would be underwater and heading for sea.

As the day wore on and Aegil's luck ran out, the wind got up and we made a fire on the beach. Aegil and Bjam took to shooting gulls again. As the hours passed, their shots grew wilder. Bjam didn't care, he was happy as long as his gun was going off. Aegil was more meditative. He really wanted a seal. It was frustrating to have come so far and return with nothing. Yet whenever the seals came back to shore, he just couldn't hit the mark.

Our time was up. It was about nine-thirty when the line boat returned from Flateyri to pick us up. The sea had a swell now and it was nice to feel nature tossing us about. Aegil and Bjam shot at the gulls all the way back to Flateyri. The fjord was like a mirror when we sailed into the harbour. The tide was right in and when he tied up, we easily stepped right onto the quay.

We hadn't got a seal but Aegil didn't seem too disappointed. I don't know what I felt. All I remember is the sight of a lot of dead gulls floating on the flat calm water.

<u>6</u>

The nights grow darker. By eleven o'clock, as we emerge from sixteen hours in the factory, the sky is grey-black with rain. It is the end of the cod quota for the summer and every ice house in the factory is stacked with cod, worms and all. Martin has found his feet, he no longer dallies to clock out half an hour after he has finished work. He goes smartly like everyone else. Yet it is hardly surprising when we start at five in the morning and finish ten or eleven at night. It makes for a long day and there are not that many Icelandic guys who stick the pace. The halibut wore them out … six weeks of nothing but halibut being unloaded off the big trawler and line boats. Those halibuts are big f…ers, too big to put through the slicing machines.

But now, it's all cod. Cod for the fish and chip shops of Britain and cod for Wendy's and Skippers and McDonald's in the States. And because the ice machine on the trawler broke down while they were at sea and the skipper got greedy and took a hundred and eighty tons instead of heading for home when he had a hundred and twenty, the cod coming through the factory isn't the best. There's to be no expensive boxes for these fishes. Nope, it's into the gyro, the quick freezer which eats them up (once the girls have filleted them) and spits them out twenty-five minutes later solid frozen and ready to be boxed. Sometimes it doesn't work out like that … the gyro gets over worked and sort of gets temperamental and has a tantrum.

Nothing serious, but it means we've all got to slow down and feed it fish at a rate of sixty. Guess when it goes in at twenty it comes out frozen, and usually if it's not too overworked, the gyro will eat them at forty. But when the cod are laid on the conveyor that feeds the machine at a rate of one a second they come out stiff on the outside and ready to rot on the inside. It's not good quality control. So, even though we've tons of filleted cod to go through the gyro, we've got to nurse the machine along.

It's the long hours and Martin's doing his bit. Despite all the vibes he gets for being a shirker, he's there with us at five when we clock in and he's there when we clock out. People again with us are starting to respect him a bit more, laughing with him rather than laughing at him. Yet people like Mike and Little Bimbo keep coming up to me.

"Is it true what he says about the counterfeit money?"

"Sure." I had heard the counterfeit money story from Martin a few times and it never changed.

"And the story of him working in a hash packing factory? That's true too?"

"Sure..." I had never been certain about the hash packing job Martin had in Amsterdam. I'd heard him tell it a few times and each time the length of time he worked there and the amount he got paid varied. Sometimes he got a hundred dollars a day ... but of course he was only working part-time ... when there were special orders to make up ... like mixing cocaine in with the hash for some high flyer.

No, I'm not saying that Martin didn't pack hash. I'm sure he did … but for how long? He's not a sticker … he can't be relied on … he's a lousy worker. All these things work against him when he talks about his past. Mike, Little Bimbo and Thori have learned to be skeptic about his stories. At breakfast in the canteen every morning, they sometimes can't believe their ears.

"I've got one and a quarter million dollars hidden away … in Amsterdam."

"You what?" said an astonished Mike.

"Yeah … it's not real."

"What d'you mean it's not real?" Little Bimbo was the supervisor's cousin. He was seventeen and spending his third summer working in Flateyri. His mother was Icelandic, his father English. He was going to school in Camden.

"See, we made a mistake."

"You mean you made it?"

"Well, a friend. He had a press. They all got bust last year and jailed. It was a ring."

"A ring of counterfeiters" asked Thori.

Thori was from Reykjavik. He was working in the summer season to pay for his last year of business studies in South Carolina. He was a smart guy and nice with it. He lived in the same house as Aegil as they'd known each other since they were kids. Whereas Aegil was tall and blond and blue-eyed, Thori was dark, stocky and brown-eyed. He was full of Viking blood and proud of it, but maybe somewhere there was early Irish settler in him. In every aspect, like Aegil, he was a cut above the other Icelandic guys working in the factory. He smoked cigars, drank cognac and played chess. He and Aegil were about even when they pitted themselves against each other at chess. Icelanders are crazy about chess.

"Yeah, see …" Mart explained. "All the notes were easy to pass off. Most of what I've got left is hundreds and five hundreds."

"Five hundred dollar bills!" Mike roared.

"Most … yeah … I've about a hundred, no maybe two hundred thousand din one hundred dollar bills, and the rest in five hundreds."

"A million in five hundreds?" Mike guffed.

"Yeah, I think so."

"You've counted it," Little Bimbo asked.

"Naw … it's in bundles of fifty thousands. They all got four years in prison."

Mike's eyes narrowed. "Did they get the plates?"

"They got the press … they confiscated it. It was one of my friends."

"You could buy a nice pack of stuff from South America with that money."

The guy who said this was Shaun. He'd been in Flateyri since the September before and as a 'bread-head' had saved five thousand pounds. The only thing that was keeping him in Iceland was his Isafirdi girl, Vika. They lived together in one of the factory houses. Mike had a room in their place. Vika was never at work any more as she was ill. She had been told to stay off the booze because her blood was too thin to handle alcohol. Whenever she drank it went straight to her head and made her crazy for a few hours. Then she'd vomit. She'd done that so often now she was ready to go into hospital. She was hemorrhaging badly. As a result, Shaun's attendance at work was two or three days a week. But he always got to unload the trawler when it came in, and that carried an extra bonus, the equivalent of two days work. However, Shaun's days at the ice plant were numbered and he knew it. He'd been in Israel before coming north to Iceland but he was heading back to England for a while before setting off for Bangkok. He was a drifter. Maybe it was the Irish in him, both parents were from, the Republic.

When Shaun got drunk, he was wild and on occasions he'd provoke fights. He was a good looking guy, probably one of the most attractive in the factory. The girls liked him, but that seemed to give him problems. Vika was a very jealous girl, insecure and frightened of losing him. She's had her two year old child taken away from her by her parents and now the little boy was being looked after by her parents who lived on an island near Akureyri. The boy had nearly choked to death at a party during which Vika had been drunk. Her parents considered her an unfit mother. But now that she was with Shaun, Vika hoped that she might have her child back. The chances of that were slim. Shaun gave out all the indications of being a good-time boy who didn't want responsibility. Yet again, what someone projects in public is usually not what they let out in private. Shaun was a dark horse.

Mike got to live with Shaun and Vika and he wasn't impressed. Mike was only nineteen, so maybe he didn't have enough insight into their relationship to see what was really happening. From the outside it looked as though Shaun was going to dump Vika and take off for Asia. The reality was that Vika was sick, she had been deprived of her child and putting all the love she had into Shaun was making her more ill.

The guy had to wise up. He didn't understand what made Vika insecure. When she grew possessive of him, he reacted by getting drunk and trying to screw whoever he could. That just made matters worse and made them argue more than they did before. Shaun had to reform his ways before it killed Vika and if he couldn't then he would have to do the bastard thing and run away. But before he could do that, Vika would have to learn to hate him. Sometimes his behaviour wasn't all that nice, especially when he was drink. Yet when the guy was sober he was affable and happy and maybe it was just his bad luck that made him fall in love with a Viking girl. They seemed suited but unless they both found a way of respecting each other they were doomed to destroy one another.

"You could buy lots of white stuff."

"My friend who had the press went to Peru," Mart said to everyone. "He took a million and a half with him. Mainly in hundreds. He's living off it. He's bought a house and has his wife and kids with him. He's coming back to Amsterdam in March. That's what I'm waiting to see. I don't want to touch that money until he comes back. Jim and I were going to pick up some of it and change it in Paris if we couldn't get a job in Iceland."

They all looked at me. Sometimes they didn't believe Mart, but they seemed to respect everything I said.

"It's true. I was desperate."

They seemed a little taken aback that I mentioned the word 'desperate'. I don't think any of them thought of me being the desperate type.

"Where is the money?" Little Bimbo asked.

"Hidden … in Amsterdam."

The work bell sounded.

"F… off!" Mart cursed.

"He always says that when the bell goes," Little Bimbo said.

Everyone piled their dishes and glasses onto Little Bimbo's tray.

"Heh, guys … I'll get charged for this."

Little Bimbo never got charged for anything because Big Bimbo was the factory supervisor. See, Big Bimbo was married to the daughter of the major owner of the company. Not only that, Little Bimbo's girlfriend Gunna was the daughter of Gunnar, the company manager and a part owner of the business.

That's how things work in Iceland.

"F…ing cod!" Mart said as he left the canteen.

Everyone else thought the same thing too.

Z

Gudmund also lives in Oddahus. He has been in Flateyri twelve years. On occasion he has left this small isolated town and gone to live in Reykjavik like so many others. Once he left Iceland and lived in London for one year, but when he tired of this, he returned to Flateyri.

What is there in Flateyri to keep a man like Gudmund here? His English is excellent and his mind is sound though there are many in Flateyri who think he is crazy. Is it Gudmund's fault that he saw the light and came to understand that Christ died for our sins?

Gudmund's ex-wife Unn still lives in Flateyri and works in the factory with her mother, two sisters and baby brother. She is dark-haired and dark complexioned which is very unusual for the people of the north-west. There is only one other girl of dark complexion, Inga, who has a mixture of French and Greek blood from her father's side. No one speaks about why Unn is so dark or why the rest of her family is so fair. She is a sensible, quiet girl and one of the most attractive in Onundafjord.

Gudmund has been committed to a mental hospital on two occasions. His mother had become convinced that he was insane as he would not let up talking to everyone about Christ. Town opinion weighted against Gudmund as the people of Flateyri had been convinced that Gummi, as they called him, had taken too many drugs too many times. The sad thing was Gudmund had given up drugs and alcohol and become self-righteous and morally incorruptible. He had been living with Unn, but after his conversion to the ways of Christ, he would no longer live with her as they were unmarried.

One day Gudmund was lying on his bed in his father's house when seven people burst through the door. The papers had been signed and they were there to take him away for treatment.

"But there's nothing flowering wrong with me. You should take a look at the people in Flateyri. Do you think they are sane? They come to me with their problems. What is all this shit?"

"Come, come, now Gummi…" One of them held a syringe in his hand.

"No flowering way!"

There was a struggle, but seven to one … the outcome was inevitable. Gummi spent three weeks in the nut house.

"Look at me, man. Do I look like the rest of the guys in here? There's nothing wrong with me. I help these guys go to the toilet, wash themselves, all sorts of things. Why are you pumping me with all this flowering shit?"

The doctor went to Gudmund's mother and told her that he thought that there was nothing wrong with her son. She found that hard to believe. If he was sane why did he go on about God all the time? In her opinion he'd taken too much LSD.

"Look, Gudmund, if you promise not to go around preaching about God…"

"Jesus …"

"Okay, Jesus. It disturbs your mother and the townsfolk."

They kept Gummi on drugs for three years. He persuaded Unn to marry him and everything went well for a while until he tried to get her to believe in Christ. She really loved Gudmund, he was intelligent, gentle and worked hard in the factory. They had their own house and plenty of the things that young people need to stop themselves from becoming bored. But Gudmund backed her into a corner over Christ. Eventually she blew up.

"I think you're psychopathic."

"Aw, Unn, not you too. Don't turn on me like this. I'm not harming anyone. Just because no one else in this town believes in Christ, am I to be persecuted for it? I know I go on, but I just want you to respect my belief, not to turn on me because you don't understand. I'm not druggy or alcoholic. There are so many sick people in this town who poison themselves with Brennivin and vodka. Am I that bad?"

They put Gummi in hospital for another three weeks. When he got out, he and Unn were finished. They still loved one another but Gudmund had pushed her too far. His tongue was too fast and lashed out too often for Unn to defend herself. She got the house until they sold it. Unn went back to living with her mother, Gummi with his father.

Since then, Gudmund's been drifting. He'll work three, maybe four days a week at the factory and the rest of his time he'll spend playing guitar or lying on his bed. Everyone comes to Gudmund with their problems, and the best thing about Gummi is that he has time for them. Unn is still obviously in love with him, but she's leaving for Keflavik with the rest of her family to start a new life. Her mother, father, brother and one sister went last week and left her to tie things up. She came to Oddahus.

"Gummi ... I'm having the dog shot."

"Hvad?"

"We can't take him with us, and anyway it's your dog."

"Don't give me that ... don't just come here and tell me that you're going to shoot my dog."

"You're not capable of looking after it. You're drunk all the time. The last time you had it, it came running back after twelve hours."

"Of course it came back. It didn't even have time to get used to being with me again. You didn't send it back did you."

"What ... to starve to death."

"Flowering hell, Unn. You know I can't have the dog with me in Oddahus."

"That's why I'm having it shot."

"Bitch! You're so flowering cold. Go on then, have it shot. If that'll make you feel better."

"You're drunk ..."

"That's right, blame my drinking for your decision to shoot my dog!"

Unn left.

Gudmund's really quite a good guy. In Flateyri he has nowhere to turn. He knows everyone and everyone knows him. Half the people think he's perfectly sane, the other half thing that he's crazy.

In Flateyri, everyone's past catches up with them. Maybe that's why people like me and Mart always have to keep moving on.

<u>8</u>

Now that the winter is on the way, it grows dark by ten, and black by eleven. It is almost mid August, and when the night descends there is light talk of ghosts and elves and trolls. In summer there are no sightings of trolls, as trolls cannot survive in daylight, they are turned to stone.

In the west Fjords there are trolls. The tales are too many and too frequently heard for them not to have some element of truth.

One late summer or early winter (for there is no real autumn in the West Fjords as there are few trees and few plants) seven farmers went in search of sheep that had wandered off during the summer grazing. As they climbed higher into the mountains, the mist descended and soon there was a high win which chilled the air and brought sleet.

The farmers lost their way in the now violent storm and sought help at a farmhouse. They pounded at the door and a great ugly man came to the door. He glared at them, and with a scowl said, "What is this? Am I not to be left in peace? I do not like visitors."

"We have lost our way," the leader of the farmers answered. "We have been caught in this storm without food and drink. Where is your hospitality?"

They shoved their way in and the ugly man neither tried to stop them nor relented to invite them in.

The farmers dried themselves by the fire. The man slid into the darkness of the back rooms and a short while later a young unhappy looking woman emerged into the light. The man stood in the doorway as the girl gave each farmer a bowl of meat.

"Eat from the side of the dish furthest from you," she whispered. "That on the near side is your lost sheep, that on the furthest, one's dear to you."

The farmers looked at one another. On many occasions, one or another of them had had a daughter or brother or some near relative mysteriously vanish. As the girl cleared the table she said, "Be careful. Are you armed?"

The farmers had their work knives.

"Don't undress or go to sleep. Remain alert, or it is the end of you."

Despite the storm it was a moonlit night. It was full and round and blazed through the sleet.

"No one is to sleep," the leader warned his men. "Lie still until I call you."

They lay down and a short while after, the man of the house came into the room. He slid up to one of the beds and felt the man's chest.

"Thin chest ... feeble," he muttered.

He felt the chest of all the others and muttered much the same thing until he reached the leader. He felt his chest.

"Thick chest ... brave man."

He turned to lay his hand on his axe and with a swing brought it down on the bed. But the farmer was too quick for him. He hopped out of bed and grabbed the axe from his hand.

"Up, my twelve men! In Satan's name!" the man shouted in fear.

The farmer chopped the man's head off and shouted. "Up my six men! In Jesus' name!"

The trapdoor had opened and out came a man. The farmer chopped his head off too. Eleven others followed and each was decapitated until there were thirteen heads lying on the floor.

"Trolls ..." the farmer said.

"Perhaps," the leader answered.

They searched for the girl and learned that she was a farmer's daughter from Omundarfjardur. She had been kidnapped by the man of the house to marry his eldest son. She had found all of them ugly and disgusting, mainly because they killed and ate people who found their way to the farm.

The leader of the farmers and one other man stayed on over the winter to look after the farm and keep the girl company. When spring came, the leader took the girl back to her father in Omundarfjardur and with his permission married her. They took all the livestock and valuables from the cannibals' farm and lied happily ever after.

A strong belief in the supernatural is common to the people of Flateyri. Elves and invisible beings live in the rocks and cliffs. Martin doesn't believe in any of that but if you can't believe in such things then what is there to believe in?

"The spirits are basically good," Gudmund told us. "Sure, I believe in them. They do favours for people. But, flowering hell, don't cross them, they can be very vengeful. They don't forgive certain offenses. I always try to keep on the right side of them … for instance, protecting their homes from damage. If some large rock or crag is to be blown away to make a road or something, a good Icelander will be out there saying, 'Heh man, what about the elves in that rock?' All over Iceland, roads have been laid around rocks rather than risking the wrath of elves."

"Legend says …" Gudmund was off on a long ramble …"that polar bears are humans under enchantment. It says that polar bears give birth to human babies, which they change into cubs by covering them with a paw."

"Come on, Gummi," Mart interrupted.

"It's flowering true, man. There was a man from Grimsey saw a female bear that was ill and brought some milk to drink. He saw that she was giving birth and took one of her young … a perfectly formed baby girl. He took the baby home and she grew to be strong and healthy. But she showed a great longing for the sea and one day she went out onto the ice in the bay. The mother bear came to meet her, covered her with her paw and transformer her into a bear cub."

Fact can be stranger than fiction and who's to say who starts lying first? Some of the stories Mart tells sound like whoppers too.

9

Now the sun goes straight into the sea about nine-thirty. The entire sky turns red and the mountains glow.

Mart and I nearly went up in a glow on Sunday when the house caught fire. Black smoke had billowed upstairs and woke us all from our hangovers. With just enough time to pull on a pair of jeans, I rushed downstairs and fought my way through the smoke to the kitchen. The plastic rubbish bin was on fire. I ran to find a bucket but could only find a cardboard box which I filled with water from the shower. I threw the water on the fire and to my amazement it went out. I reached through the smoke for the kettle and finished the fire off.

Meanwhile Martin was out the back door trying to get the fire extinguisher to work.

"Forget it, Mart."

"Eh ..." He peered through the kitchen window. "Oh yeah ... it's out."

He went back to bed while me and Paddy, a boy from Kerry, spent three hours cleaning the kitchen. It was a mess. The walls were black and the lino on the floor was burnt and charred.

"Jesus, that was a near thing. The whole house could have gone up."

"Someone's thrown a cigarette into the bin ..."

"Holy mother, that could have been me," said Paddy.

It could have been me too. About three in the

morning, pissed on wine, I'd emptied an ashtray into the bin. Who knows for sure? It could have been Ricci.

Ricci was one of the town drunks. He was the nicest of guys when he was sober but once he'd had a few bottles of Brinnavin, his eyes rolled back in his head and he became a walking zombie. The night before the fire, Ricci had come to the house in his regular weekend state … blind drunk and ill-tempered. Without fail every weekend he ends up in a fight, and who's to say that all these fights have not contributed towards his unpleasant looks. I mean when he's sober, he's got the nicest smile and his eyes hold a twinkle. But once he's on the Brinnavin, his jaw drops, his eyes swell and he gawks at everything. The Icelandic boys in the house … Beggi, Vidar, Godmund and Kiddi, always end up throwing him out before he starts picking a fight. As usual they'd ask him to leave … he'd refuse … and they'd have to man-handle him. Kiddi's done him in a few times because Kiddi's a right little Viking. But see, Ricci never seems to learn … every weekend it's a repeat performance.

On Saturday they threw him out of Beggi's room (which is the party room) and locked the door on him. Next thing they knew they could smell burning. They opened the door and found Ricci had set fire to the paintwork with his lighter. They grabbed him and tossed him down the stairs (which is no easy thing as Ricci's a burly guy). But as usual, Kiddi sorted him out, and Ricci went wandering off looking uglier than ever. I'm not saying I saw any blood. Nope, I'm not saying that.

When he's sober, Kiddi's a nice guy too. As an Akureyri boy, he thinks that the people from Isafirdi are snobbish and stuck-up. It makes me want to laugh as there are only three thousand people in Isafirdi but I guess I've seen a bit more of the world than Kiddi who's never been out of Iceland.

Kiddi's hobby is speed. He's the main fork-lift guy in the factory and drives his fork-lift faster and better than anyone else. He also owns a red V8 super charged TransAm and is the fastest guy on four wheels in the whole of the Western Fjords and everyone knows it except Kiddi who can't see how fast he is going.

Kiddi's a little guy with dyed blond hair and he's all muscle. If ever there was a real Viking left in Iceland, he's the one. At weekends when he decides to party, he puts on his leather outfit and drinks until he goes berserk. Sure, Kiddi's got drink under better control than most of the other Icelandic guys. He can say no and stay sober when he wants to. But when he lets go, he lets rip. Maybe because he's a small guy he feels he has to prove something, but nobody else feels that he has to. In a way, the younger guys admire him for his driving skill while the older guys like him because he's like a little kid and never gets seriously bogged down in the shit in the factory. He does his job and does it well and no one complains that he doesn't pull his weight. Sometimes he's reckless when hauling fish out the hold of the trawler with the crane. It can be kind of dangerous loading half a ton of fish on a pallet and having Kiddi lift it out when he's in a reckless mood. You kind of hook the clamps on and as Kiddi jerks it up at about fifty miles an hour you get out the way in case the whole lot comes down on your head.

But at least Kiddi isn't a sop-faced little bastard. In fact there aren't any of those in the factory at Flateyri if you leave out Magnus.

No. Kiddi's a good guy. He's pretty level headed. He has to be when he's driving his TransAm.

"That thing can shift," said Mike.

Mike was a sucker for cars. He'd written off a sports car, a Mercedes and a pick-up and he was only nineteen. Guess that's the privilege of being a rich kid. He was dying to get behind the wheel of Kiddi's red V8.

Kiddi's driving was in a different dimension from Mike's. Kiddi spent a fortnight's wages just to buy two new tyres for his car. As soon as the tyres were on he was burning rubber up and down the streets of Flateyri. There are only three streets that run the length of the town and the middle one is a dirt track. So to burn rubber in Flateyri you drive up the street that runs along the harbour side of town and come back on the tarmac street that runs along the back of the town on the seaward side of the fjord, or you can do it in reverse. Whichever way, it's about four hundred yards of surfaced road.

Kiddi knows every centimeter of it … he's driven it a hundred times. Lunch breaks. Evenings. Weekends. He's out there racing up and down doing tail-spins and wheel-locks and tyre-burns. The guy is so fast that he did the nineteen kilometer dirt-road mountain run to Isafirdi in nine and a half minutes. Most people are lucky if they can do it in thirty.

Kiddi's been making so much noise and causing such alarm with his V8 that the town committee have put concrete and metal barriers in half stages on the harbour road and back road. They just appeared one day. The Twins (who do all the road and public building maintenance in town) came along with these barriers and placed them in situ one at a time with their bulldozer hopper. Eyebrows were raised, questions asked but no one would admit why barriers were suddenly needed across the road. Neither of the roads went anywhere except out of town towards Isafirdi and at the other side of the town the factory was four hundred yards away jutting out into the fjord.

Everyone knew why.

It hasn't stopped Kiddi who now uses the barriers as chicanes. The wheels still spin, the tyres still burning. Well, at least they sort of do. On Sunday after cleaning the kitchen, which now has black walls and a burn in the floor as big as a coffin, Martin, Paddy and I went and played some pool at the Vaginn (The Wagon), the local hang-out. I got tired of being beaten and went to see Mike who was still in bed with a two day hangover. Suddenly Omar and Kiddi burst into the room.

"Have you seen this trick, mother f...er?" Omar was half Icelandic, half American. He was nineteen and mixed up. He lived in the same house as Mike and Shaun and Vigga. He was a wild one. When he got drunk he got good mother f...er drunk.

"Come on man, look ..."

"Yaw ... nice trick ..." Kiddi's English wasn't so good.

Kiddi held a plastic bag of water up in the air and Omar struck his lighter and held it against the plastic.

"You bastards ... don't do that in here." Mike was wanting some peace and quiet. I was sitting thinking about Ricci and his setting fire to Baggi's door and the fire in the kitchen. They say things come in threes.

"See man," Omar drawled drunkenly, "it don't burn at all."

"Get that bag of water out of here," Mike snarled.

Kiddi laughed and started to leave the room with the bag but Omar grabbed it from him.

"You chicken mother f***er. You pussy."

Omar threw the bag at Mike and the water went all over his bed. Mike threw the bag off his bed and the water went all over me.

"You shit. I'll get you for this. When you're out I'll go into your room and pour water over your guitar and amp."

"You try, you pussy, and you'll die at nineteen."

Omar had a strange sense of humour that sometimes seemed harsh. I'm not saying that he's warped, he just likes to bait people to see how far he can push them. Mike was too scared to grab Omar by the throat to get him to show a bit of respect. Omar was bigger and stronger than him and anyway Mike was no toughie, he was a soft rich kid who'd had things easy in life.

Omar locked himself in his room just in case Mike did have the guts to throw water on his guitar and his amp which were his main source of pleasure after booze.

Kiddie felt sorry for Mike. He was drunk like Omar, they'd been drinking since Friday afternoon but he was holding it better than Omar.

"Mike, you drive car …"

Kiddi showed Mike the keys to the V8.

"Okay, are you sure?" Mike wasn't one to turn down the chance of driving Kiddi's car. And anyway, he owed him for the bag trick.

"We go furir … dive."

Mike got dressed and the next I saw of them was when I was back at the Vaginn watching Mart and Paddy playing pool. Sure, I hadn't seen them but I'd heard them. Everyone had heard them screeching up and down Flateyri through the chicanes doing spins.

They pulled up at the Vaginn and saw that Mike was at the wheel. Kiddi was in the passenger seat and Little Bimbo in the back. Mike had one arm leaning out the window, an arm that was all scraped and bashed up from Friday night when he'd been sitting on the bonnet of Kiddi's car and Kiddi had pulled off at fifty miles an hour and rolled him in the dirt. Mike had to take Saturday off work as he had torn his knee and was limping. Shaun and Vigga had cleaned his wounds with vodka (which when you think about it is a pretty generous thing to do when alcohol is so hard to get and so expensive in a place like Iceland).

"Kiddi's teaching me how to do tail-spins."

"Oh yeah," Mart said with a knowing smile.

They pulled off.

"I wonder if Kiddi knows how many cars Mike's written off," I said.

"What do you think the life expectancy of Kiddi's car is now then?" Paddy asked.

"Kiddi's a good driver," Mart said.

"He should be a rally driver now," Paddy said. "He's wasted in a place like this. He could be making a living from it."

"He shouldn't let Mike drive his car," Mart said.

And sure enough Mike drove the V8 into a fork-lift down by the factory.

"It was Little Bimbo's fault. He was saying, 'Go on. I want to see it spin.' So I put it into spin and suddenly Berni was in front of me with a fork-lift. I put on the brakes, the car veered to the right, and if we hadn't clipped the fork-lift we'd be in the sea."

"Was the fork-lift okay?" Paddy mused.

"Those things are like tanks," Mart said.

"The fork-lift's fine," Mike said with a raised voice. "But Kiddi's car's a write-off."

Mike didn't seem to be too bothered that the car wasn't insured and that he had no intention of paying for the damage to the car. We all felt kind of sick about that. Kiddi was a nice guy and the car was the one thing he lived for. It was his hobby and in half an hour, a rich kid had done his hobby in. People play with fire and others get burnt.

10

I am a mere mortal on this Earth and it is not of any consequence that I can name five major moons of Uranus and that I can point to two of them in the darkness of the Arctic night.

No, there are more important terrestrial matters to concern myself with. Star gazing is the occupation of a dreamer. For the now Uranus is beyond the reach of man, and man must, and will, continue to concern himself with earthly matters.

But what of earthly dreams? Martin, it seems, has no dream. His vision of happiness changes with his moods. For a while he has been waking up and going to work in a contented manner. At least I think he has come to terms with the strangeness of Flateyri and the strenuous nature of his employment. Once more, I have begin to like him and take his side in humorous asides or petty discussions.

Then like the wind, his mood changes and he is back to cursing the world. Once again he finds an excuse for unhappiness – a cold, a bad task in the factory, the lack of time to eat his canteen breakfast. Once again he plummets into dismay and vile fits of temper. Once again, he is shunned by all, and by me and I wonder if I can continue to share a room with him much longer. Once again, he starts going to sleep at ten or eleven in the evening and as part of the process he locks the bedroom door on me. Sure, we have to compromise and find a balance but most times I don't feel like going to bed at eleven, and most times

I'd like the option of being able to sit in the bedroom reading a book or thinking with the light on.

"Bloody kids! Bloody noise! Bastards!"

This was the extent of his utterings when Gudmund or Beggi or someone played their stereo loud or had friends round or used the toilet. Mart's bed is right next to the toilet wall and he has the habit of banging on the wall after eleven o'clock when someone uses it.

"Bastards! Hurry up, you wankers!"

It kind of disgusts me. Mart's turned into an anti-social being. He comes home from work and locks himself in the bedroom until it's time to eat or someone's hired a video from the Vaginn. Then he'll spend time in the kitchen or the lounge but as soon as eating's over or the video's done, he's back in the bedroom and asleep. Maybe the work wears him down but it's more likely that he just isn't happy. I thought he was getting better but his relapse has left me in despair.

"I'm getting sick of your moods."

"Fuck off!"

I can't even reason with him any more.

"I think you should go and ask Aegil for a room of your own."

"Oh, you think so, do you?" His tone was sarcastic. "Don't you think I've thought of that!"

"Why don't you do it then?"

"Fuck off!"

Martin couldn't help himself if he tried. I mean, how can a guy who's done as much as he has be so useless. I had been thinking earlier in the week, during breakfast at the canteen, that out of all the people at our table – Mike, Little Bimbo, Shaun, Vigga, Claire and Mart – I would rather be stuck on a desert island with Mart than any of the others. Then later in the week, with his bad moods and filthy attitude back, I reckoned I'd rather be on the dessert island alone than with Mart. Maybe, I'd take Claire, for despite all her mixed up faults of not being sure whether she was a woman or a man, underneath all the confusion, there was a decent person.

I couldn't say that about Mart for I'm beginning to know that Martin isn't half the guy he makes himself out to be.

"He lies all the time. God, how that guy lies," Claire said to me in the kitchen one day. "I wish he'd say nothing rather than lying."

Claire and Mart still had phases of getting on well together, then periods of heating each other. As for us, I could see the problem was mainly Mart's. He only wanted Claire for one thing and that's the one thing she wouldn't give him.

"She's a cow … a bitch. I hate her. I'd kill her."

"C'mon Mart, nothing's worth going to jail for."

"She is. I'd do it. I would."

Mart's threats were never said to the people they were meant for. It goes back to him being a coward. He'd never say something like that straight to someone's face. "You're a bastard." He'd slip it in in an aside that you wouldn't quite catch. He'd mumble something and you'd see him looking sheepishly away.

"What was that?"

He'd always answer, "Nothing."

Then you'd know for sure that he'd said something like "Cunt" or "Bastard" or "Get fucked." See, that was the extent of Mart's conversation now. It was almost as if he'd got so chocked up that the only thing that came out any more was obscenities and hostile thought. Where was the Mart that had made me a wooden chest at Cothelstone? Where was the good time Mart that didn't care about anything but having a good time?

Now it seemed as though the whole world was on his shoulders. He was more miserably than Claire. At least she laughed from time to time and did little things for people that showed her caring side. But Mart did nothing for nobody. He was as selfish and as uncaring as anyone I'd ever known. Well, maybe I've got the guy all wrong and the problem is me. I give him a hard time verbally for being such a slacker at work. Sure, he's working harder than he used to, and doesn't hang around to clock out any more, but still, if there's a job to be done that requires team work, nobody wants to work with Mart. Well, with the exception of Paddy.

Paddy and Mart have struck up as buddies, or so it would seem. In fact, it seems that Mart has latched on to Paddy's Harris Tweed coat tails. Maybe that's not such a bad thing, we all need friends, and Mart sure needs one badly in Flateyri. He and I have been growing apart since we got here. I guess Paddy will find out about the lying and everything else and deal with it in his own way and no doubt Mart will unload all his resentment of me on to Paddy. It's only nature, we've all got to let go now and then and I suppose I'm as much a bastard as anyone else. I've got into running my big mouth while I've been here ... out of boredom who knows ... and my tongue is sharpest when I use it on Mart.

I shouldn't be the one to cut Mart too harshly when he's shirking work or off loading responsibility on someone else, but I hate it when he lies and I can't stand it when I see him trying to get someone to do his work. He's such a sly bugger and such a compulsive liar it's hard to tell when he's actually telling the truth. I used to be able to tell but I've been wrong so many times, I don't know what to believe any more.

See, Mart's like a little kid who's permanently doing wrong. Like I said before, when you ask him something, his initial reaction is always the same.

"Heh, Mart. Do you want this?"

"Yeah ..." he answers immediately and then he thinks about what you've offered him and then sometimes detracts. "Eh, on second thoughts ... no, it's alright."

See, if he thinks that you're offering him something with no strings attached, he instinctively says "yeah" first, then he decides whether he wants it or not afterwards.

"Heh, Mart, did you ..."

"No!" he'll answer before you've even finished the sentence. He believes that people are permanently accusing him of doing wrong. After a while, you come to realise that Mart feels persecuted all the time, that people are trying to prove him wrong, to out do him, to rip him off, to put one over on him. All that flashes through his head in an instant and then when he realises that you're asking him whether he'd been to the shop or done his laundry or played pool, he'd answer, "Yeah, did that …" But ask him if it's his dirty pot in the sink or has he clocked out or how he's feeling, he'll lie.

No doubt Paddy will find all that out because Paddy, despite being an uneducated boy from Kerry, is not dumb. See, Paddy's got a dream, one of the most beautiful dreams I've ever known someone to have. It's a dream that I could easily foster myself and carry with me as a barrier against the futility of man and his ways.

We live in such a transient world that all our problems will be nothing when we're dead and gone. Uranus and her five major moons will remain and so too will Paddy's dream. With such a dream, a man or woman could not help but love the sort of person who harboured such a beautiful notion in their head. For despite all Paddy's human failings, despite his unwashed ways (he maybe showers once a week and always smells of fish), despite his human weaknesses for alcohol and cigarettes, despite his vegetarian diet (except for duck, wood pigeon, chicken and turkey), despite his inability to turn in for work every day, despite his frail constitution and pallid complexion – Paddy's dream is his redemption.

We were icing fish.

"I shouldn't tell you now …"

"Go on, an … you're saving for something."

"Let's just say I'm saving for the future."

"So you'll not be spending it all in a week in a bar in Limerick."

"I will not. I'm going to plant trees …"

Suddenly his secret was out.

"I'm going to plant trees on this bare hill I know in Kerry. I've been saving to buy the land off an old farmer boy. All I want to do is plant broad-leaf trees and watch them grow. I have to start now that I'm thirty or there'll not be enough time. I just want to watch them grow … oak, birch, beech …"

Why hasn't Mart got a dream like that? Why haven't I? I'm no better than a hobo like Martin. I'm going nowhere and doing nothing. Mart wants the money for his nose operation. I want it to pay off my credit cards. Where's the dream in that? Where's the future in money? Where's the everlasting in a Visa bill? I guess I haven't got a hope even though I do know the names of Uranus' five largest moons.

I may dream but I don't possess one.

11

And the rain pours down. Perhaps there is an autumn in Iceland after all. There are trees though. There are not many in Flateyri. But there are one or two in the garden of Husith, the new house in which Gudmund and the Icelandic factory boys have moved to. And in out of the rain stumbles Gudmund. It's Tuesday night but he's drunk and looking like some weirdo from the sixties. It's black outside but he's wearing shades and an Afghan coat. To complete the outfit he's got an old white shirt wrapped round his head. He stumbles into our room where I'm alone. Mart, Paddy and Claire are playing pool at the Vaginn.

"Gummi, what's the shirt for … to keep the rain off?"

"No flowering way, man. It's to attract attention."

"This is a small town … and anyway everyone knows you. They'll be saying 'There goes Gummi with a shirt on his head.'"

"Let them, man, they know me. I know them."

Gudmund sat down. I was lying on my bed. I'd been listening to the rain. But perhaps you, reader of this narrative, want to know more about life in Flateyri. In many ways it is just an ordinary little town with very ordinary people. There is nothing in Flateyri to set it above other towns in Iceland. In most countries, Flateyri would barely pass as a medium sized village and who for the life of them can say how many tens of thousands of villages there are like

Flateyri in Northern Europe.

Yet when I think of the people, I remember that it is people that make each village different from the next. Any hobo can tell you that. Each village may have a church, a store, a post office and houses that all look the same but the faces there are different. Maybe this seems all too obvious but how else can I get it across that nowhere else is like Flateyri.

"Flowering hell, man. I need someone to talk to."

He'd come to see Claire who he'd had a two month affair with before Mart showed up. They had been in love. Claire told me so.

Maybe I want to show you Gudmund in a good light and try to hide the fact that he's a little mixed up. I mean, he's not crazy like some people try to make out, he just gets drunk. A happy man doesn't go on a week long binge.

"I know it's just a phase I'm going through."

"I still can't understand what keeps you in Flateyri, Gummi. A guy like you should be in Reykjavik."

"Reykjavik?" He looked at me. "No way, man, my mother lives in Reykjavik. Anyway I spent last winter there."

At this point I thought he was going to stop but he was ready to talk about his whole life there and then.

Perhaps I shouldn't let you in on this conversation, there are some things which should remain confidential. But why f***ing not? Half the town knows more than half of what's going on anyway. There was no doubting that half of them already knew that Gudmund was wandering about town with a white shirt on his head.

"When I was young ... eight years old, my eldest brother was the apple in my father's eye. My father raised him up to be just like him but he was killed hunting when he tripped and his rifle went off. The bullet travelled level with the ground, hit a rock and came back and went through his head. Father then took me as his favourite but I could never replace my older brother. My parents split up and my father brought me with him to Flateyri.

My other elder brother had left home but my youngest brother Vikingur lived with my mother in Reykjavik. When he was younger he always wanted to fight with me but I was three years older than him and it was always easy for me to put him in a headlock or something. Ten he went to Australia and joined the Australian army. When he came back to Iceland he was massive. The first thing he did when he re-met me was take off his shirt. He wanted to fight me. This was in my mother's house in Reykjavik. We pushed back the furniture, I took off my shirt and we would have fought if some friends of my mother's hadn't stopped us. Vikingur is massive, you've never seen such a guy. He's always fighting and he always wins. At a dance or something he'll go right up to guys and knock them out cold.

He's crazy. He killed my mother's boyfriend. He punched him on the nose and the bone broke and went right into his brain. He went to prison for a year and he's never been the same since. He blames my mother for her and father splitting up. He's horrible to her and now mother wants me to go back to Reykjavik to look after Vikingpur as she can't cope any more. I can't do that, man. I told her that. She wants me to take over the apartment and care for my brother who's been in and out of mental hospital. None of the institutions will have him any more as he's too violent. I told mother that she can't run away from it, it's her son and she must face it, not pass the problem over to me. The tenants in the apartment block have got a petition up to keep Vikingur out of the building. Mother has had the police throw him out a number of times.

Now, Vikingur sleeps at the police station. Uncle Bubbi has tried helping him but he's so busy being a pop star he hasn't the time to look after him either. What can we do? My mother wants me to go to Reykjavik, my father wants me to stay here though he thinks I'm crazy and lazy. That's why he threw me out of the house. No warning, nothing. I was living in the basement, just playing my guitar and he burst down the door and ordered me to leave."

Gudmund had told me all about his father before, and how he can never quite live up to his father's expectations of the perfect son. Gummi knows he's just a stand-in for his dead brother and he can't cope with his father's disapproval of him. He and his father once had a fight. Gudmund had been at the town hall dance and two guys had threatened to beat him up. He went outside with them and laid them both out. Gudmund's father had come forward to help his son but Gudmund had laid him out too. The cops showed up and wanted to take Gummi away for the night but his father insisted on taking him home. The townsfolk crowded round and the cops released him. On his way home with his father they started arguing. They fought and the cops came back and arrested Gummi. They released him in the morning. His father was waiting at the front door with a rifle and wouldn't let him back in the house.

That was years ago but his relationship with his father still seemed to be on a short fuse. Gummi's drinking didn't help nor did wearing a white shirt as a headband.

Yet for all his craziness Gudmund is not crazy. It's such a shame to see such a good looking intelligent guy turning into a lush. He showed up for work on Thursday morning, one week after he'd just clocked out to go on a bender. "Heh, Mr Brinnavin! You're back!" shouted Paddy from the crow's nest of the trawler. "Gud dai, mate ..." He walked up the gang plank as if he'd never been away.

In a way he hadn't. We all lived in the same little town. It was just a relief to see him off the drink and back at work.

We'd been painting the trawler all week. It was laid up for the week as it had used up its fishing quota. The crew had gone off on holiday, half to Florida, the other half to Istanbul.

We had over two hundred tonnes of fish to

process, but we'd been out of fish a week now.

Working on the trawler was a welcome change from fish.

12

It is still raining. The mountains are half covered in light snow. Autumn has definitely arrived for the road over to Isafirdi has been impassable in the evenings.

And so August ends and September arrives. We have been painting the trawler all week, me, Mart, Paddy, Skalla, Vidar, Runar and sometimes Shaun. Mike got sent back to the factory for being a lazy bugger. He ran his mouth and forgot to paint at the same time. Disa, the ship's painter from Isafirdi, has a way of handling us guys when we get out of line. Mart, bored with painting the stern, in a lapse of concentration dropped his brush into the harbour where it bobbed up and down close to the hull. He slid down the trawl-slip and spent half an hour trying to fish it out. Eventually he untied the paint raft from the quay and paddled himself out and regained the brush.

Three-quarters of an hour later he was back painting the stern with primer. A while later there was another splash and this time Mart's paint can was adrift in the water. Once again he descended on to the quay, got on to the raft and paddled out. But this time, he was well and truly adrift and happy to float out to the middle of the harbour.

"Mart's floating away!" shouted Shaun.

"Let him be. Let him drift!"

"No … you can't leave him," Shaun replied.

"Why not," I answered. "Let him go."

"No," said Shaun, rushing off to throw Mart a

line.

Typical Shaun, he hated work too. He went off to play with Mart. It was twenty minutes before Mart was on the dock. Disa, who'd turned a blind eye to the brush, issued a command.

"Martin ... I want you to go downstairs."

"Eh ... me? The sun's shining."

"Downstairs ... and help Skalla."

Mart was sent down into the fume reeking newly painted hold.

"I don't think he's happy with me. I don't think he like me now," she said.

"I'd send him home."

"You don't like your friend?"

"He doesn't like working."

"No ... he'll be okay downstairs."

Disa was a nice woman. I didn't have the heart to tell her that Mart had thrown his can into the water, not dropped it. But at least she'd noticed that "MART WAS HERE" daubed in grey primer on one of the bright red trawl-slip walls.

"Your friend ... he goes with you when you leave here?"

"No way. I'm leaving him behind."

"Oh ... I thought he might be going to work with you in Scotland."

"No ... he's going to spend winter here."

"Is he?" She raised her eyebrows. "And what are you going to do in Scotland?"

I had an idea of what I wanted to do. See, I hadn't lived in Scotland since I left there when I was seventeen. I thought, yeah, maybe I could give it a try, live close by Jack in Banchory, spend the winter in the Highlands. It sounded okay, and no one in Iceland seemed to think it odd that a Scotsman was going back to Scotland. It just seemed sort of strange and new to me.

"You'll not settle there," Mart said over a game of pool. "You'll be off somewhere. You'll end up back in the States."

I just couldn't rule out that possibility. I had planned to go to the States to work and visit friends but I'd ended up in Iceland instead. See, in many ways, I'm no better than Mart. I've been making Mart out to be a serious sort of guy but really I'm the serious one. Mart's more like Peter Pan, he hasn't grown up yet and doesn't want to. Watching him fish for the brush and then the can gave me belly-ache, I laughed throughout the whole farce … but the way I tell it, you'd think that Mart was incompetent. The thing is, Mart knows what he is doing most of the time. He's not completely crazy and he's not all coward. Earlier in the day, he'd tight-roped a hawser to pain the highest point on the stern with primer. Neither Vidar nor Runar dared to follow him later with the grey over-coat. As a result every time I see the grey primer on the very top of the stern, I think of Mart.

Painting a trawler is no easy job. Sure, it's better than working with fish all day long, but when you climb up the ship's sides and hang over a hawser to paint a rusting panel, one slip and it's a broken back or neck. I guess I've had lots of jobs like that so that it doesn't scare me very much, but there's always at least one scary moment … like being in the crow's nest sixty feet up, hanging on with one arm and one foot, a paint can in one hand and a brush in the other, and a stiff breeze blowing the paint into your eyes which you can't wipe away as your hands are full. You can't let go of the can or there's paint on everything that's just been painted. You can't let go of the brush or you've got to climb all the way down then all the way up again to start again. It can be no fun but the feeling of freedom from cheating death is fantastic and I wouldn't trade the risk for the world.

See, we don't get paid any more for taking risks. It's all part of being alive and competent. I know Mart would climb the crow's nest and hang out there all day if he was allowed. It's the sort of thing that appeals to him. It's not boring. Boredom is Mart's greatest fear in life. It's one of my fears too and I'm sure we're not the only guys who feel that way.

So, there we have it. Have what, you may ask? Well, when it comes down to it, Mart and I are both running away from something. Can I put my finger on it? Sure I can but should I tell you? I think you should be able to work it out for yourself but I guess some people would prefer to have it straight from the horse. Truth is, Mart and I are scared of being caught up in routine, the same sort of steady monotony that kind of creeps over everything you do. Maybe there's comfort and security from repetition, you've done it once and it gets easier every time you do it. But you get to a point when it becomes so easy it gets hard to do it. I mean they physical task becomes so simple that your mind goes dead or it starts to fight. You end up saying to yourself, "I'm not going to do this shit any more." I guess that's when people start cracking up. They become dissatisfied and restless. That's what happens to Mart. Only difference between him and me is that routine gets to him quicker than me. He always wants to change what he's doing.

So, now Mart's gone off to Reykjavik for a few days with sixty-five thousand kroner in his pocket. That's about enough to live on for two months in England and four months in Asia. But in Iceland that won't even last four days, not in Reykjavik. Everyone tells you that ... I haven't been there but it sure isn't difficult to spend fifteen thousand kroner on a night out in Isafirdi which is a little town with nothing but dancing and alcohol. Hit the bottle in Iceland and you can say goodbye to all your savings. I'm going nowhere near Reykjavik until I quit Iceland. But Mart couldn't wait. The money was just sitting in the bank burning him up. He just had to get it in his fingers and be good to himself.

Nothing wrong with that but I guess that's why he'll be here until next Spring. I'll be long gone. There isn't anything I could find in Reykjavik that I can't wait for. Mart just doesn't like waiting for anything. Whether it's his breakfast or it's a woman, he's got no patience.

And now that he's in Reykjavik do I miss him?

Yeah, I suppose I do, I've got used to having the guy around. It's been more than three months since he showed up at Cothelstone. That was the beginning of summer and now summer's gone, lost. And most of it's gone missing in Iceland, vanished in hours of work.

But I guess it's not over … the sun still waits until eight-thirty to go down over Greenland way. The light lingers until nine then drops off like the mountains into the dark of the fjord. Up until that hour I sill get the chance to read my letters by the window. Letters that tell me that VISA are going to give me my card back and that my bank overdrafts are a thing of the past and that I'm in credit. Letters from dear friends. Letters from old lovers, and from Gilla.

Remember Gilla? We met Gilla in Lerwick, far distant Lerwick in the long dark free days of June. I have written and she has written and I have written again and she has not yet replied. And do I really expect her to? I cannot hope for that, she is happy with her boyfriend in Germany, and I am on the fringes of the Arctic wilderness. Yet she is a flame that burns bright while I am in isolation. She is personification of what I cannot have in this, my exile.

Why must I think of my time in Flateyri as exile? Perhaps it is because I miss the comforts of home and friends and all that settled domestic life gives in the way of contentment. Here in Flateyri I am only content if I work long hours and get paid more than the week before. Only in financial reward is there contentment. Each wage takes me closer to freedom and escape from the slavery of debt.

And Mart? In Reykjavik? He is not a slave of debt, he is a slave to pleasure. Yet while he's in the big city chasing alcohol and girls, I get to sit by my window and watch the whole sky turn red. Even the sea glows red. And into the sunset glides the Gyllir, Flateyri's trawler, our trawler, the one we've proudly been painting all week, its bright red and white striped hull slipping out to Greenland and bearing north-north-west to the Arctic fishing grounds. At such a sight I am glad to be in Flateyri under the red night sky, the glow of the northern world, far more than I can ever be in some land closer to the equator. I am a northern world boy and in my heart and soul this is what I shall always be.

For despite the remoteness and isolation of Iceland, as a Scot, Icelanders are my neighbours. And yet if Mart heard me say this, he would say that I have no neighbours, I have wandered too far and wide to believe in such triteness. These would not be his words to express such an idea, but this is what he'd try to get across to me with a "bullshit" or a "rubbish".

But Mart's not here and I have my thoughts to myself. I have our room to myself and that is nice. For once there is a stillness and a calmness and an easiness that doesn't exist when Mart's around. There is a freshness, an openness and a peacefulness.

Perhaps I am deluding myself but things are different and I like it.

13

How can I explain half of what goes on to someone who can have no idea of what it is like to live in a small town on the frontier of nowhere. As I've said everyone knows everyone else and their business. Sure, the girls try to be discrete about their late night visits on guys but everyone gets to know what's going down. See, in Flateyri it's the girls who do the bed hopping and the guys have to wait for it to come to them. I guess that's the way it's done in Iceland thought I can't tell for certain as I haven't had the action anywhere else.

I'm not going to brag for there isn't anything to open my big mouth about. But I can tell you one thing. When new people show up in Flateyri everyone checks them out like meat. One look, and everyone has decided whether the meat's worth eating.

It seems that the women are worse than the guys. They are sheer wolves, nothing less than hungry animals ready to hunt anything. And I mean anything!

The same can be said for the guys. They'll fuck anything and I suppose I'm getting around to thinking the same damned way. If they're over fourteen, then they're old enough to say no to. I've never met so many horny little girls in my life. They'll come straight up to you and ask you if you'd fuck them.

Shit, you're saying, this is pure filth, but hell, it's the whole truth. Why should I lie? I'm the one living this and this is how it is. I'm getting laid and Martin isn't.

Poor Mart. Hell, I suppose I shouldn't feel sorry for my mate. He got back from Reykjavik after four days on the bottle. The sly bugger hadn't told me that he knew a girl in the big city. He'd met her in Israel while working on a kibbutz. That was ten years ago. But Iceland's a small place. He tracked her down through the telephone book and she came in her car and took him to her place. Whether he made love to her or not I don't know. Mart hasn't said anything about her which makes me think that she was probably married with three kids. But Mart's a dark horse, he probably had his way.

One thing's for sure, Reykjavik cheered him up … when I got back to the room after work, he was pissed on vodka.

"I was nearly killed, Jim … do you know that? Skalla was drunk and drove off the road and we ended up in a ravine. It took the police two hours to pull us out."

"Where was this?"

"Two hours after we left here."

"Was the car a write-off?"

"It was all smashed on the outside and the inside. The seat-belts wouldn't work any more. But it still went and we drove on to Reykjavik. Shit … I was scared. Bloody Skalla!"

"Where's he now?"

"Still in Reykjavik. I flew back today. I spent all my money. Bought a CD player, a sweater, an electronic chess set."

"Electronic chess set?" I didn't know that Mart

played chess. "Let's see it."

"Oh, the chess set ... it's at the kibbutz girl's place."

Mart is always like that. His women don't have names, they have titles. His wives are the Australian one or the Brazilian cow or something like that.

"I borrowed twenty thousand off her to buy the chess set."

"You spent even more money?"

"I'll pay her back, I've still the money in the bank. I'm staying the winter, see, it'll not take me long to save again."

Mart was trying to convince himself but from the way he was laughing and smiling, blowing more than a thousand pounds in three days had done him a world of good. I couldn't help feeling that he'd got laid too. He just seemed more relaxed and like his old self, the self I'd known at Cothelstone.

"There's been some changes here ..."

"I can see that ..." he laughed.

Summer had returned, glorious blue sky and bright yellow sunshine. But that was only a temporary change and not what he was alluding to. I had to fill Mart in on the changes at Oddahus.

Two Swedish girls had arrived in Flateyri looking for work the same day Martin went to Reykjavik. I had just finished work and was pissed on vodka that Gulli, one of the big bosses (Bimbo was married to one of his daughters) had given us for doing such a good trawler painting job. The girls were in the Vaginn and had nowhere to stay so I said they could have Beggi's old room in Oddahus until the factory office opened on Monday.

They were pretty girls, though I'll tell you now, that after so long in Flateyri, even an average girl seems beautiful. I don't know what it is but even the least attractive women in the factory become passable. No, I don't know what's happening to my head. One thing is certain, Flateyri is not full of beauties! Maybe it's the fish, maybe it's that I just don't get to see the pretty ones. Yet something tells me, now that all the kids have left, something in the back of my head which is akin to a memory tells me that there are good looking girls in Flateyri. Everyone goes on about Reykjavik and I guess that's where they've all gone. I wonder what the girls think of us ugly looking guys.

I don't seem to be getting anywhere with my tale about the Swedish girls. But bear with me. Once I kind of let you know how psychologically important these two girls became, then you'll maybe understand why all hell broke loose when they left again after five days.

It was a disaster. Bloody Claire!

Mart was back and everyone in the house was in a good mood. There'd been no fish all week and an army of girls had been sent into Oddahus to clean and paint the house. The place was transformed, we could hardly believe it. We could see our faces on the walls. The Swedish girls had been told they could start Monday coming. Still, they were bored out of their heads doing nothing. They were ready to party and have a good time and the whole household was up all night. There were some other new arrivals. Monica, a girl straight up from Cape Town and Kevin, a boy from Newbiggin-on-Sea in Northumberland. There was lots of flirting going on and everyone was high. Mike, Paddy, me and half the Icelandic boys already had the Swedish girls number one and two on our conquest list. I'd invited them to Mike's for dinner the following night and Mike already had it in his head for them to move into his place as Shaun and Vigga had left for England. I'd never seen anyone so happy.

Then, while we were all at work, the girls fled back to Sweden. At lunchtime Mart met them at the post office waiting for a ride to the airstrip. He couldn't get much sense out of them but something had scared them.

"It was that witch Claire. I hate her!"

Martin was right. Miserable bloody Claire had got them in the kitchen and screamed her head off at them. Why? God knows, but she's a scheming bastard. No sooner had the Swedish girls gone than she had Monica out of her room and into theirs. Claire had been instructed by the office to share her room with Monica and hadn't liked it. Now, she'd found a way out of it.

Mart was furious. We were all mad, so mad that Claire had to lock herself in her room. What had she said to those girls? They were so happy when they went to bed the night before. The Icelandic guys went crazy when the found out. Omar wanted to get a petition up to get rid of her. Kiddi wanted to string her up by her tits. Nil wanted to break down her door and throw everything she owned out of the window.

I moved out of Oddahus and into Mike's. I'd had enough of Claire. Sure, I needed my own room, my own personal space away from Mart but the deciding factor was Claire. I couldn't stand her any more. She was a bitch as Mart had said all along. I'd tried to give her the benefit of the doubt. I'd try to see her side of things, her way of looking at life. She'd be nice for three days and that would be fine. Then she'd turn nasty for a day and I'd have to say, "Heh, Claire, can we have a truce? I don't like being nasty back."

"Nasty," she'd say. "What do you mean? If you'd get to know me you'd find out I'm nice."

"Not when you're nice for three days then nasty for one. It undoes all the nice things and just makes me want to tell you to fuck off."

"But I'm nice," she'd scream.

At moments like that I knew the girl was in cuckoo land. In our own way, all of us are nuts, but Claire is nuts in such a vindictive cutting way she leaves me feeling nasty and uptight so often. I can't be bothered with her any more. The thing is, Claire has to stay sweet with me as I owe her twelve hundred pounds. She'd given me more than 100,000 kroner during the devaluation scare a month back and I'd sent it to England to have it changed into Sterling. The kroner never got devalued but I got a shitty rate in England that was almost fifteen percent down on what it should have been. It wiped a hundred and eighty pounds off the value of Claire's money.

That made me feel bad but she'd asked me to do it for her so it wasn't my fault. Now she wanted the full value back but there was, or should I say, there is no way I'm going to be the loser on a favour. It was her risk at the expense of my good intentions. I've lost out too much in the past and I'm not going to this time. Not to Claire. No bloody way!

So now I'm at Mike's place, a small three roomed wooden house off the second street … I don't get to see the sun going down any more but I get laid.

<u>14</u>

The summer is lost for good now. The days are wet and the nights are damp. Darkness falls by eight-fifteen and the wind whips up the sea. The gulls come in to shelter from the squalid weather. It is rare to see anyone in the street. The kids are all back at school and the town is devoid of life, deserted. The rain beats down on the derelict house across the street. The road is awash with mud. The cold begins to bite. Winter's not far off. Snow is coming.

"You'll never guess what happened."

Mike had had two girls the night before. They'd knocked on the door the usual Icelandic way. The first one, Helga, had shown up about one o'clock in the morning.

"I was giving her … you know … a bit of … and she stopped me and said, 'What are you doing? Ain't you going to give me one?' I said, 'I'm giving you some foreplay,' and she said, 'what's that?'"

"You've never had foreplay before. These Icelandic blokes must just be on and off. No wonder you've come round here!"

No foreplay Helga was notorious. She'd been with nearly every guy in the factory. She'd had her quota for the summer before she had to go back to boarding school. She was only sixteen.

Inga had been Mike's second visitor. She'd knocked on the door about four o'clock. Mike had thought to send her away but, shit, what the hell. He invited her in. As long as he promised not to tell her boyfriend, she said he could do what he liked. Mike had never even seen her with a boy and did what he liked anyway.

Inga was seventeen, or so she said. She was really only fifteen and a half. That half over fifteen made all the difference. She was really dark, her complexion was not snow-white Icelandic. As I said before, she had a mingling of French and Greek blood from her father's side. Unn was the only other Flateyri girl with a complexion as dark and sultry.

Inga was a randy little thing. Like Helga, she got about. the night before, she had given it to Omar who had also given it to Usa. See, I keep trying to tell you what Flateyri's like.

But, hell, I'm giving the town a bad name. That's not fair. It's the best little town in the whole world and I'm not going to say one more thing against it. Even Mart has stopped cursing the place. He's getting settled for winter. He's thinking positive. He's weighed everything up and he can't think of anywhere else to spend winter and save at the same time.

I guess he's right. I can't think of many places where you can get by on doing so little for so long. I mean, sure you could be on the dole but you wouldn't be putting away two hundred pounds a week in the bank. I know money isn't everything but there's nothing else to keep foreigners in Flateyri except money.

I'm not staying for winter. My feet are itchy. Time moves on too fast and if I stand still too long I feel as though my time in life is going to be up before

I've done a thing. Nope, winter in Flateyri's not for me. Don't get me wrong. I could hack the snow drifts and the blizzards but I've set my mind on going back to Scotland for winter. I miss having a close relationship with a woman I love. I reckon the odds are against me finding a woman who's going to love me before the New Year, I've had my quota for my year. But shit, I can hope and I can only try to be myself and that's usually enough. I can't do much more than that and if that doesn't work then it's fate.

Gilla hasn't replied to my second letter so I guess I won't be going to Germany or get to see her again. That's life. Sometimes it's impossible for the traveling type of guy to bridge the miles. There are too many miles and too many stops on the way. Sometimes I feel as though my emotions are all over the place. A girl in New York, another in California, one in Wales, another in England. All of them this year and yet I try for one more in Germany? I'm crazy and I'm nowhere because I'm with none of them.

I'm in Flateyri slowly working my way out of debt. At least Mart can dream about what he's going to do with his money (if he doesn't spend it all in Iceland). I've got nothing like that. All I've got is the notion that if I need money to set myself up some place else like Scotland then I'll have to get the money.

It's a vicious circle, but maybe being in debt is also an incentive to work. Too many people want to make a profit out of life, someone else has to take the loss. It's basic economics and I'm not going to be a greedy bastard. There's far too many greedy bastards already. There is enough cake for everyone. When I meet someone who tells me there's not enough cake to go around, I make sure they get none of it. I say to all those bastards who tell me that you have to look after number one – go fuck yourself, I want nothing to do with your pretty screwed up world. If some bastard says to me that you can't trust anyone then I sure as hell don't trust them.

See, I hate negativism and I can't stand people who feed you with warped values if there's something in it for them. I call them crows and that isn't being fair to crows. The crows just sit out there with their big black eyes waiting to eat. They know a carcass when they see it. They know when they're getting something for nothing. They'll wait until you're dead. You can't ever expect any help from a crow. It's not in a crow's interest is it?

Mart's got a bit of a crow in him. Maybe Mart's more like a magpie who picks up shiny things. But Mart will help people when they're down. He'll let them borrow money and he'll offer them a cigarette. Sure, he was tight with his cigarettes when we first started in the factory but now that the lean times are behind him, he's feeling good with himself and more willing to give.

In many ways, Mart has changed while in Flateyri. He's happier. The local people are still a little wary of him but in the factory everyone's joking and talking to him more. Mike, who has always been one of the biggest mockers of Mart, now talks to Mart as if he's just another one of the guys. Not always but sometimes.

Yet Mart's best mate beside me (I haven't been much of a mate over the last few months, but things are better now that we have our own rooms) is still Paddy from Kerry.

Paddy can't make up his mind whether to stay for the winter or go back to Galway. Paddy can't come to terms with returning to Ireland and going on the dole and receiving twenty-five pounds a week. Where is the future in returning to the past? Mart has put it into Paddy's head to see a bit of the world. Now Paddy's dreaming of taking the cheap train from Budapest to Peking across Siberia.

And what do I think of that? I think it's great, as long as Paddy still plants his first dream … trees. All the traveling in the world cannot amount to anything. It amounts to nothing. One tree … just the thought of planting a tree fills me with greater joy. For when you are in the Wets Fjords of Iceland, you begin to long for a stroll in a wood or a hike through a forest. You crave for the scent of fire wood and the stillness of its coniferous canopy, the sensation of softness underfoot and the silence of the sap dripping and the needles dropping.

I miss it. How I miss it! The protection of nature. For here in Iceland there is no protection from the elements. There is nothing between the foot of the mountains and their peaks. Nothing but craggy, rock-face mountains. It's not ugly, the mountains are majestic and beautiful in their own supreme way. But there is nothing to break up the stark contrast between the dark of fjord and the white-capped hills. There are no soft lines.   The fjord ends and the mountains start. The only thing in between (and only in a very small and insignificant way) is Flateyri. The rest is wilderness, untamed and unused barrenness. Tufts of grass, a few rare mountainside plants, lichens and moss and then nothing but igneous rock and snow.

This is the Iceland of the West Fjords. This is the Onundersfjord. A few sheltered valleys on the southern shore, a few scattered forms, standing sheep and nothing more. All other life is on the wing or beneath the waves. And without the creative life beneath the waves there would be no life on the land.

The Onundersfjord survives on fish and that's why Mart and I are here.

<u>15</u>

There is a blizzard raging. A week left of September and we are cut off from the rest of the world. The whole valley is white and shrouded in snow clouds. The wind is fierce and cold and biting. Winter has come but I still want to believe that it is summer.

The money's bad, we've had no good catch for weeks. A seventy ton load of Pollock, cod, haddock and catfish doesn't keep us going all week unless Bimbo eeks it out. Our pay is so poor, we're making little more than half of what we earned weeks ago. It means we're working forty hours, no overtime, nothing. That's okay but because everyone's got so much spare time on their hands, it makes them bitchy. Especially the foreign women.

I guess when I count them up on my fingers, there's eleven foreign girls in the factory, six from South Africa. They're a mixed bunch and basically okay people except for the odd tantrum or weird mood.

Claire's the strangest. I've told you about Claire before and I guess there isn't much else I can add. She's still the least liked of all the people in the factory. Gudmund likes her but he's still in love with her. Claire's got no friends in Flateyri. She's a loner though you can tell she'd love to be the centre of attention. Everyone wants to be the centre of attention sometime or other. It never happens to Claire even when she gets drunk and loosens up. She's still too much like a man and that turns everyone off. It's not that she's a horrible person, it's just that she has a communication problem. Maybe there's a language barrier and she has to translate everything she's thinking in Afrikaans into English and something goes missing.

In this respect she's like Mart – what Mart thinks is not what comes out of his mouth. At least when Claire says something that is a downer, she usually means it. It's her kind of humour – insult someone and see how they react. Usually she gets a negative reaction and a returned insult that shuts her up. It's a crazy way to communicate with people. The end result is that everyone gets wound up and tense and that leaves no one feeling good.

No, Claire's at her nicest when she says nothing and smiles. She's got a pleasant kind face when she sees the good side of things. But it's her eyes, her dark brooding piss holes that look as if they want to kill you. Sometimes a look of puzzlement comes into them, almost as if she can't quite understand what you're trying to put across. At these moments she seems slow and vulnerable and I feel some sort of pity for her. That never lasts long … the soft look of puzzlement disappears and a vindictive dagger of sharpness comes back to her eyes. More often than not she'll flee away with a parting insult that cuts no ice with anyone. Well, not with me. Sometimes it leaves Mart or Shaun cursing her.

"Bitch … f***ing bitch. I could kill her!"

Mart's got a string of off-pat insults that sum up what he thinks of Claire.

"I hate her … the dyke!"

Mart always has to bring Claire's sexual preference into his insults. It dents his macho ego that he lives next door to a lesbian. Truth is Claire thinks that Mart is a dumb, slow witted liar.

"I'm too smart for that guy. I don't believe a thing he says. He's fucked up."

"She's the one that's fucked up," Mart will tell me.

And so their love for one another is mutually lacking despite their early closeness. Guess that's the way it sometimes goes with people. The factory would be quite happy to let Claire go back to South Africa, no one in Flateyri has a good word for her, except for Nina at the post office. Nina and Claire get on alright together and perhaps it shows that maybe there is a nice person under all the confusion that Claire creates. I'm sure she's a nice woman but only if she can rid herself of her hostility. She's an unhappy soul and off-loads her misery on everyone else. That's how she gets her kicks. She's happiest when someone else is more miserable than herself. Maybe that's why she works so hard on making everyone else so unhappy.

Claire's on a loser. Someone who destroys happiness to create their own ultimately is ostracized. No one in the factory will sit with Claire at breakfast. She has a table all to herself. I'll say, "Good morning," and she'll say, "Good morning," back but no one else will say a word to her. In the house it's slightly different. Shaun will talk to her for a while and then cut the conversation short before she gets to him. He tries to communicate with her. Mart doesn't even try. He'd sit and mouth insults behind her back. He'll mutter something that no one can quite catch but something that is understood to mean.

"She's a lesbian cow!"

I can't handle Martin's antics any more. It's childish behaviour which just adds to the tension. With two new lesbian girls in the house he's getting worse. It's hardly surprising that Martin's disliked by all the girls. You can't go around snickering behind people's backs and expect them to laugh it off and like you for it. Maybe Mart doesn't worry about being liked but I've never known anyone who really wants to be hated.

"I'm growing to hate that guy."

See, Claire has feelings, and Mart makes her life even more miserable than it already is. They make each other miserable.

What's wrong with Martin? Maybe he feels cheated that he's come all the way to Iceland to share a house with a bunch of lesbians. He doesn't see these girls as people, he sees them as sexual objects. Or at least what's what he projects.

Why has he such dislike for girls who prefer other girls to boys?

I suppose the world is full of prejudice and that it manifests itself in everyone in different ways. In Mart it is plain. He is sexually prejudiced. I don't know how he can ever think that any woman could be his equal and more. Women are a threat to him and he negates the threat by putting them down, by degrading them. Maybe that's why he's been married five times and not stuck with any of them.

I can't say that Martin treats women like shit but I suspect he does. A woman is tits and cunt to Mart. There's never any talk about their minds.

"No woman with half a brain would have anything to do with him," said Claire. "He'd bore them."

Maybe she's right, maybe she's wrong. Mart's my mate and I've got to take his side on something. Mart's not boring, he's just … well, he's not all there any more. Too many drugs or something over the years, I can't say what. Yet when he drinks a bottle of vodka or rum his brain just goes to mush. It's almost as if the good part of his brain which is left goes blank. He's just done too much of everything in the past … mushrooms, LSD, cocaine, nitrates, hash and booze. Maybe he gets on well with Shaun because Shaun's a simple guy looking for a simple life. Mart with all his experience has turned into a simple guy too, a guy who's happiest playing Scrabble or pool. These are the things in Flateyri which give Mart the greatest pleasure. He and Shaun have bought a three thousand piece jigsaw and spend hours piecing it together. It's something they can share, something they can see their time going into. In the end they'll have something to show for their leisure time. With Scrabble and pool there's no record of where their time went.

Shaun's not interested in girls very much. Mart was interested in the new arrivals, Anna and Kate, until he found out that Anna and Kate were a couple.

Anna and Kate are from Cape Town, like Claire, Monica, Cynthia, Jackie and Carol. (I've met more South African girls in Flateyri than I did in Joburg when I met Mart.) I haven't got anything against the girls but it is kind of strange that so many South Africans are being employed in Flateyri. There's not many countries South African's can go, never mind places where they can work legally. The only other place is Israel. Sometimes they can get to work in England but everyone knows that England is one of the countries that's keeping apartheid going.

Anna and Kate are nice girls. They're part of the exodus that's been streaming out of South Africa for the past fifteen years. They want to see the world but the world's against them seeing it. I can't blame the world and can't blame Anna and Kate for being South African. Like Claire, they're Afrikaners and that's no advantage to anyone outside South Africa.

Anna and Kate are madly in love. They are inseparable at work, in the canteen, at home. Anna is tall and dark and strong. Kate is small and blonde and fragile. They'll sit on the sofa in the Oddahus lounge, Anna's feet up, legs apart, Kate resting on her shoulder, her hand sweetly massaging Anna's vulva.

It's cute but it's driving Claire crazy. She's got the hots for Anna and no one can see anything but trouble from that. She hangs around Anna fussing and smiling and touching and Kate is such an innocent, easy going girl that she thinks Claire is just being friendly. But we all know what Claire's like and pretty soon things will come to a head. Anna and Kate will have a tiff and Claire will be in there like a shot coming between them. But Claire doesn't stand a chance. Anna and Kate are so devoted to one another that the end result will be that they'll ostracize Claire the way everyone else does. It's inevitable. Claire is just one of those people who makes enemies of everyone.

And then there's Monica, who had to move back to sharing with Claire since Anna and Kate arrived. Everyone seems to have forgotten the affair with the Swedish girls except Monica who has it at the back of her mind. She's not too happy that she has to share with Claire, it's bad enough having her in the house. Sharing a room with her is misery. Monica handles it well. She has fended off Claire's advances on her and now that Claire is making a play for Anna and got bored molesting Monica, she's being left alone.

Monica's got beautiful flashing eyes that fascinate me. She has a sensual way of looking that makes me want to make love to her, which I have. She's twenty-two years old and that's not that old. Five months in England as a nanny for a wealthy Suffolk family and she didn't have one boy. Now she's making up for lost time. I guess I've been too flighty for her, slipping away from declarations of love and the sort of things that go with romance.

"She's fat! I wouldn't fuck her," declared Mart one day at the top of his voice. None of us listen any more to Mart's comments on women. I like Monica. I like talking to her, and making love to her is a warm and passionate experience. I can't be her boyfriend. I just don't feel that way. I just can't walk up and down the streets of Flateyri holding her hand like Gudmund can. For it's Gudmund she's turned to now and of course, besides being a man, Gudmund is a very warm human being. He can give Monica more than I can and I'm sure he does.

"I've got to talk to that boy," blurted Mike.

"Talk to him about what?"

"He's sinking lower and lower. After Unn, how could he even consider being with someone like Claire! And now Monica!"

"He looks for the good in people, Mike. There's nothing wrong in that. Being with Monica will make him happy."

"I've got to talk to him ..."

He never will. Mike might talk to Martin or Cynthia about Gudmund, but not to Gummi. And Cynthia would say something to the point.

"It's sex. What else could it be? There's no such thing as love. I don't believe in it, it's all hype. Woman and man get together because they have needs and in Flateyri that means the weekend when everyone's drunk."

Cynthia, good old Cynthy, how I love her too. She's got a big, big heart and a very loud voice. Cynth has to shout, it's her way of being centre of attention which she is more often than not. If I was to describe Cynthia I would say she's like a crow! Claire's like a jackal, Anna like a mare, Kate a rabbit, Monica a hen. No, that's not fair on any of them. Cynthia is a bundle of joy. She sometimes reminds me of a puppet without strings, like Pinocchio. There is something sweet and cute about her, something that makes her irrepressibly buoyant and happy.

But her moods! Wow! It must be the Irish in her.

I cannot continue, it pains me to think of her when I am leaving.

Yes, I have snapped. I have had enough of work in the factory. Too many things have suddenly just dropped into place. And even though this evening Cynthia came to see me, I couldn't tell her what I am about to do.

I am running out and I am taking Claire's money with me, every penny. I am going to rip her off and I don't give a damn. See, out of the blue, Irene who has just flown in from London, has given me her return air ticket. The flight is on Saturday and it's now Thursday night.

It's all for free and will save myself more than three hundred pounds. I'd be a fool not to go and an even bigger fool not to take Claire's money. I haven't told Mart yet but I can just see the grin on his face.

"Good on you, Jim. Serves the silly bitch right!"

16

How can I get across to you how I' feeling right now?

I feel great.

I have lighted out of Flateyri and I'm in Isafirdi waiting to fly to Reykjavik. I told Claire at breakfast in the canteen that I was going to hitch to Isafirdi in the afternoon to get her money. Sure, I've hitched to Isafirdi in the snow but I've got all my bags with me.

I am elated.

Three months in Flateyri, over. Three months which were a lost summer.

But what a summer!

I liked Flateyri and I liked everyone there except Claire. I've never met such a bitch in my life. If someone had told me that someone else could be as nasty as Claire, I'd be skeptical. But now I know for myself. I mentioned to Mike and to Mary-Ann and to Mart and all three encouraged me to rip her off. There is probably not one person in Flateyri who will sympathise with her when it's discovered I've run off with some of her lolly. Certainly not Omar, or Kiddi, or Nolly. Certainly not Cynthia, Monica or the other girls. Certainly not any of the foreign guys. Maybe Gudmund will shake his head a little and lower his opinion of me. Certainly Anna and Kate will sympathise with Claire as they haven't seen through her yet. Maybe the guys of the office will raise their eyebrows and tut a little. But that will be it. Behind her back, everyone will laugh and then within a few days it will be forgotten as everyone becomes caught up in some other drama. And when they speak of me, Jim the guy who ripped off Claire, they'll say that "it was a mean thing for me to do but she deserved it." What else will they say?

Flateyri is frontiers-ville. Anything goes and at the end of the day, money is the name of the game. I've made my money and I've managed to get out. I don't have to stay for the winter like some of the other poor suckers. My trip to Iceland has been a success.

Mart has to stay on. At lunch time, during the break, I had him over to the house and told him what was going on.

"I knew it! I knew you were going to use that ticket!"

"I'd be crazy not to. With Claire's money, there's a difference of fifteen hundred pounds if I stay."

"I'd do it."

What can I say? I've had nothing but encouragement from friends in Flateyri. Take the money and run. I'm foot loose and drifting. I haven't got a home and only a vague idea of where I'm going next. My friends in England think I'm in America. My friends in Iceland think I'm going to Scotland.

So where am I going? Sometimes I think I'm worse than Mart then he reassures me that I'm not. Just this morning before he found out I was leaving Mart was talking quitting and spending winter in Goa.

"In Goa!" I exclaimed. "You change your mind all the time. Don't go to India again. Use that money and have your nose operation. Then get yourself to Australia. Unless you do that, then shit … what's the point of staying on here?"

"I might leave in a couple of weeks." He laughed. It seemed that he was even surprised to hear himself talk like that. Up until then, he'd been so sure that he was staying for winter. "I'm missing girls. I wish I was in Amsterdam. I'd have a good time. All these weird dykes here. They'll drive all the guys here away."

He was right. There is very little to do in Flateyri, and if there is no sexual interest, then there's no interest at all. Claire had been talking about getting her gay friends in Cape Town jobs at the factory. Anna and Kate had begun writing to their friends with the same message.

There isn't anything wrong with homosexuality, male or female, but in a small place like Flateyri, half a dozen lesbian girls would use up the foreign single girl quota and there would be no one to keep the hard working guys warm. In a place like Flateyri, sex is very important. It's important everywhere in the world, but even more so when you're in a remote fringe where there's only one pool table, one sun bed and nothing else for recreation. People want to play Scrabble and cards and games like that but only with people they get on with. The lesbian girls Claire, Anna and Kate do not mix with anyone else. Claire spends all her time strutting like what she thinks a man should strut like. Her whole personality makes the other girls nervous of her. Only Cynthia and Irene are strong enough to tell her to piss off. The others live in dread of being accosted by this randy overbearing he-she.

Maybe this is the root of Claire's problem. Everyone would love her to pack her bags and go home to Cape Town. Instead of her leaving, she's driving others off. She got rid of the Swedish girls and pretty soon she'll get rid of Mart and Paddy. In a way, she's got rid of me, except that she's had to pay me to go. If I hadn't got her money, I'd have stayed a few weeks longer to make up some of the difference. I would have had to.

So I'm in luck. In a way, I am also a shit. Until yesterday I had every intention of paying her back the money I had accepted from her.

And now? Well, now I guess I'm just like most people, I'm dishonest. Yet if I'd liked Claire, I could not have imagined running off with the equivalent of ten weeks savings for her. But that's all it is. Ten weeks that she shouldn't have had and now hasn't got. I tried to tell her ten weeks back that she should go home. She didn't take my advice and asked me to bend the currency regulations for her and send the money to England. Firstly I accepted the money as a month's interest free loan and secondly I did it as a favour. Well, I haven't done her a favour and now I have a free loan. Maybe she'll catch up with me and if she does I'll cough up. I'll probably cough up spit first, then the money.

There now, my guilt is passing and my time of departure from the West Fjord is drawing close.

So where am I going? All I know is that I'm on my way to London. After that, who can say? Like Sitting Bullshit ... (the name the Icelandic boys have coined for Mart) the world is my home. Wherever I go, I know everything will work out. In Flateyri everything worked out just fine.

Incredibly damned fine!

I'm a shit but at least I'm a happy one. I guess they'll give me my credit card back now. Goodbye lost summer.

As for Mart, there was one last thing he said to me just before I left.

"Tell mum, I'll write ..."

"You'll never write!"

"I'll write ... maybe a Christmas card."

We parted. I knew I probably wouldn't see Mart again for a long time. But I guess that's the way it is sometimes with brothers. Despite all the little things I hated about him, I loved him. It's not everyone who has an older brother who's been to a hundred and fifty countries and been married five times.